THE BLACK EMERALD

Novellas and Stories
Jeanne Thornton

INSTAR BOOKS • NEW YORK

Cover by A. Litsa
Book design and illustrations by Jeanne Thornton

Assembled in the United States of America
Second Digital Edition

ISBN (paperback)   978-1-68219-908-4
ISBN (ebook)   978-0-9904528-0-5

10 9 8 7 6 5 4 3 2

TABLE OF CONTENTS

PUBLICATION CREDITS

Some of the stories in this collection first appeared in other publications, as follows:

Energy Arcs and Fractal Skies	*The Evergreen Review*
Skeleton	*Night Train Magazine*
Tomato Plants	*The Medulla Review*
Satan in Love	*A Capella Zoo*
Chairs	*Santa Clara Review* *& Fiction Circus*

Dedication
is overrated

I. THE BLACK EMERALD

PROLOGUE

ON REAGAN'S FIRST DATE with Josephine, the two girls went to the theater on Lamar Street where you could order food that was bad for you while you watched movies that supposedly weren't. Reagan and Josephine ordered thick, fat shakes made with caramel and salt, and they split an order of fries with green chili queso, which they munched happily as the credits began. The movie had been made somewhere in the Middle East, somewhere depressing that you heard about on the radio, and although it was a cartoon it was in black and white. Its hero, Reagan guessed, was a little boy who was making a tree out of scrap concrete and wire in the cratered field outside the house he and another family shared in the refugee camp. A crew of animated animals began to cavort around the tree: a boar, a hyena, a goofy pelican, a wise old scorpion that resented the poison in its tail. The animators from wherever this was were talented, and the black lines defining the outer extension of the animals squashed and stretched in perfect sync with the action. The animals kept urging the boy to build his scrap tree higher, higher. Meanwhile, in the house, the boy's father, who spent most of his days fishing in the oil-and-war-polluted sea, clashed with the boy's brother, who'd recently been recruited into a group of fanatics of some stripe. There was a nice scene where the boy's brother gave him advice that was not age appropriate in a Wes Anderson kind of way, then spoiled the ironic effect by telling him that dreams were the only thing that made life worthwhile. The dreams thing really ruined it.

Reagan assumed the end of the movie would be depressing, but Josephine had taken her hand (Reagan guessed out of some kind of ecstasy) during a particularly long vignette where the boy trailed laborers on their daily commute across a border, the whole time asking the laborers for scraps and packaging for his tree, and the two girls made out through the final forty minutes and a hunk of the credits. Reagan unbuttoned the two buttons of Josephine's blouse just below the top, slid three fingers inside her shirt, let her skin slide along her breastbone, felt her head swim as the soundtrack filled with Foley gunshots and jarring music. This was what it felt like to be in love, she knew; stories told her so.

The last shot of the movie was the scrap tree in the field outside the charred ruins of the house, requisite silent cuts of each dead member of the family still smoking like meat. The animated scorpion was slowly burying his dead animated pals around its roots, his sad, stoic eyes on long, frail stalks. In the white light of the final credits Josephine smiled and smoothed her hair and buttoned the blouse and Reagan sat with her hands on her lap.

And although she had no wish to believe it, this was the first moment Reagan started to believe that there was a way out of her ordinary life. The way lay straight through love and through Josephine. Josephine rose like a great wave before her, a wave so navy dark it looked black, and if Reagan could wait in one place, feet on some strange surfboard with the perfect balance of tension in her muscles and perfect attention to every shifting current in the water that surrounded her, Josephine would swoop beneath her, lift her, carry her someplace far away, someplace where she could feel the sun on her forehead.

1

REAGAN ALWAYS HAD TO look when she dialed Josephine's phone number on the virtual keypad of her cell phone. She sat on her knees on her bed, her head propping her blue woven blanket up like a tent, and the backlight of the phone made a tiny campfire inside; her own breath made it hot.

Josephine didn't pick up. Reagan bit her lip and dialed again. She dialed a third time. Josephine would pick up if Reagan just kept dialing.

What, Josephine said, picking up. Her voice was always higher than you expected. The great joy of loving a girl completely was that you always kind of knew how her voice sounded on the phone, but still you got to experience it every time; all the perfect details that the brain filtered out like they were caught in the mesh of a sieve but that passed easily through tiny fabric speakers.

I just needed to call you, said Reagan.

You can't just call me, said Josephine. You know that. We broke up.

He's downstairs, said Reagan. He said it was her own fault if she felt like a prisoner in her marriage, and then he just broke a glass or something. I don't think he threw it. It was a kind of quiet shatter. I guess he dropped it. I guess that's better.

I don't want you to do this again, said Josephine. This isn't my problem to solve for you.

He's calling her worthless, said Reagan. He says she's the reason he was never able to succeed at anything. His self-pity is really luxurious right now. It's really piquant tonight.

You're making this my problem, said Josephine. This isn't a fair thing to do.

Reagan bit her lip and closed her eyes: the nasal voice of her father rising as he got angrier, falling then rising again as he moved from room to room, the level mumble of her mother apologizing to him. If Reagan could become carrier waves and travel with the signal to the satellite then back down to the world, she would find Josephine sitting in the dark of her room, maybe on the floor by her bed, her neck supported by the soft corner of the mattress and comforter. She would have a book half open in her lap, or a magazine, or the remote on the little DVD player she had in her room to watch important serial TV shows; she had been doing something before Reagan had called, interrupted.

I want to come over to your house, Reagan said.

You can't come over, said Josephine. I broke up with you. It's going to be a while before we can be normal.

I want to lie in your bed again, Reagan said. I want to kiss your neck. I want to put my hand on your stomach. These aren't unreasonable things.

I can't give you these things, Josephine said. You need to respect the boundary I'm establishing.

Fine, Reagan said, and she hit the virtual button that hung up on Josephine.

She sat there under the blanket holding the phone away from herself, watching the glow of the screen until the power saver made it fade and turn dark and all she could see was the faintest reflected edge of her knees, the chopped curls of her hair. When she got it cut her father said she looked like a Depression moppet, an Orphan Annie. He liked reading books about the Depression. She wished she was an orphan. No, she didn't. That was a fucked up thing to think. She didn't want to think fucked up things about the world. The world was a really great place, really, if you just understood why everything happened the way it did, like God could probably.

Her father's voice was swelling again. I think we can work it out this time. I think we can try really hard and maybe you can be more supportive of me and maybe I can be more willing to accept support from you. I think this can work. She could imagine her mother's eyes, wet. It would be quiet for the rest of the night.

She took the blanket off her head. Her room was still there, motionless: her thin shelf of anime volumes, her action figures with dust on their feet long set in heroic poses, her Scotch-taped posters of green-haired girls wielding crystal swords facing unfathomable dark forces that looked like smoke, her boots lined up perfectly even against the door as if an orderly ghost might be preparing to march through the wall. She went to the drafting table and turned on the swivel lamp. Her Rapidograph in hand, she drew long, curving lines that found their way toward one another and formed a cartoon picture of Josephine. The long rectangle of a lapsed-Mormon jaw, blond bangs cropped close, ridiculous headscarf pattern of black and white hypnotic spirals, melting eyes. She had drawn Josephine many times; Josephine always said Reagan made her look ugly, made her jaw and shoulders look enormous. She tried very hard to fix these problems as she worked.

When she was close to done with the drawing, she tried calling Josephine once again. This time there was no answer. Reagan listened to the song Josephine used as her voicemail—a quiet, classic 1980s neo-psychedelic thing, movie soundtrack material. She closed her eyes and nodded her head to the backbeat.

§

Her parents were asleep; she sat on the floor by her boots, all her music stopped and trying to keep her breath quiet until she was one hundred percent certain that they were really asleep. Then she crept out the door and went straight to the curb, stood there looking into the blue blackness under the street light. She had to look when she dialed Josephine's cell phone, but her feet knew the way to Josephine's street by heart, and they led her there like the entranced victim of a vampire.

Josephine's lights were out. Reagan watched them for a while, and then she lay down in the street besides Josephine's sweet sixteen car. She made sure to lie on her side so that someone could see her arm from the house. After twenty minutes she got up, made a show of brushing off her jacket, and went into the middle of the street to lay down instead, stretched out across the concrete. But it was a school night, and there were no cars this late and this far from the city, and after another ten minutes she got up and walked home.

§

She finished the drawing of Josephine's shoulders, bare, angel's wings from the blades, light radiating in blasts from her skull. *I will keep you*, she wrote on the page in letters wrapped in snaky vines of ink. She sat in the tall drafting chair looking down at her pen point as it leaked black ink at the outer edge of the heart, one of whose lobes was taller than the other, imperfect, imprecise.

§

She woke up to the sound of her father knocking on her door. She could imagine him there: short, balding, eyes big and brown and vulnerable. In one of her cartoons he would be the screaming victim of a titanic monster, the kind of uniquely ugly face that it's too complicated to draw episode after episode, so it's best to have the character killed early. It's more convenient for everyone.

The garbage, he said. The garbage, Friday morning.

I'm sleeping, she mumbled. I'll do it later.

No, you'll do it Friday morning, he snapped. Not later.

He was saying something more to Reagan, something about how she had to respond, to confirm that she'd take out the fucking garbage Friday morning before school, no later, that this would constitute an oral contract between them so he would know he could trust her. She scrunched her eyes tight and made a ball of blankets in her arms, held it to her, imagined it was Josephine's head, Josephine who could save her.

2

MISS STEVENS WAS THE cool teacher, hair dyed heather purple and flapper cut with fat amber jewels that rested on the moisturizer-smooth expanse of chest just above the neckline of her gypsy's blouse. She liked the Dresden Dolls and Neil Gaiman stories and she openly had a girlfriend whom none of the students had ever met. Miss Stevens had told them all about this girlfriend on their first day of class—some jerk had asked her if she was married, what a jerk—and Reagan had basked, then, in this aura of having-a-girlfriend they had in common.

At the beginning of the year Miss Stevens had required each

of her students to sign up to meet with her in her office so that she could interview them about what their intentions had been in signing up for an art class. She was trying to get to know each of them, she said. During Reagan's interview, she'd sat opposite Miss Stevens's desk on a department-issue plastic orange school at one end of the office, a wide space containing dull steel cabinetry bearing magnetic words that formed clunky inspirational messages, posters of woman-positive musical acts, a fat plush rabbit with different pushpins and paper clips stuck into it for easy access, mugs with Sailor Scouts printed across them, stacks of perspective studies from freshman Intro Design students, Miss Stevens' foil-stamped Outstanding! stickers deforming their outer corners. Miss Stevens sat down in her beige rolling chair with the psychedelic blanket hanging off the back. In the corner a massive ficus belched oxygen into the room. There was a big jar of pretzels laid out for Reagan; she helped herself.

I want to be good at drawing comics, Reagan said as the interview began.

Miss Stevens smiled extra wide.

Bravo, she said. I'm very much a fan of comics. Who do you like? Do you like manga?

I don't know, said Reagan. I've never read much of it.

You should, said Miss Stevens. Have you tried drawing comics? What have you drawn comics about? What are your stories about?

I guess people being happy, said Reagan, after thinking about it for a while.

People being happy? asked Miss Stevens.

Yeah, said Reagan. Like how in movies, a lot of times, when it starts out, people are happy, you know? Like take Uncle Scrooge. At the beginning of a story he's the richest duck in the world. Then he tries to go after, I don't know, a diamond or a chest of gold or something like that. Eventually there are all kinds of complications and problems, and the treasure turns out to be some kind of terrible mirage, or even if it isn't some kind of terrible mirage it's far more trouble than it's worth to get. He takes all kinds of pills and nerve tonics, and it's all because he chases treasures. If he'd only stopped and looked around and what he has, he'd think, hey. This world is pretty good after all. It's a feeling that a lot of comics don't seem that interested in exploring. It'd be boring, said Miss Stevens. Exactly. I agree with you.

Reagan frowned, but it was important that her art teacher like her, so she adjusted what she believed.

§

When Miss Stevens said that it was a mistake to use a true black, like an out-of-the-can black, when you were making a painting, that it was far better to mix different colors to produce your own black, warmer or cooler based on your feeling and your eye for mixtures, Reagan stared at the zebra-striped clip that held back Josephine's bangs and guessed she maybe knew something about how the black you thought of depended on your feeling. Right now if she were painting Josephine—she could do it from memory if she had to—she'd use a green and brown black, as if the fields of color that marked shadows on Josephine's neck were being seen from the bottom of a pond in a forest, algae and dust swirling in the water above Reagan, and she had to swim as hard as she could, straight up, to get to Josephine, up where the air was and all. And she figured if she was flawless with the way she swam she could make it back, too.

Black was relative. You had to harmonize your blacks. You had to use the right black for the right situation.

During the work period she sat and listened with half of her brain to Josephine asking her tablemates if they thought the colors popped enough on the hipster models she was X-Actoing from ads. With the other half she scissored out neat panels from the Harmon Metzger comic book she had on her desk.

§

Her best friend forever Peter was infuriating, but was good about letting Reagan come over at any hours, all hours, to sprawl on his bed or his futon, whichever he wasn't using, to read his comic books, to blather about Josephine until his eyes closed and he'd claim he had been thinking deeply about the situation after you woke him up and yelled at him. Peter was transgender, female to male; he'd just joined their class this August at the start of the school year, Reagan figured because he'd had to move from some previous school after he came out. His parents never talked about why they'd moved; both were professors who were deep into some useless discipline like linguistics or American studies; Reagan never listened when they told her about it. Peter's family never ate together, which wasn't strange to Reagan—like her parents ever ate together—but they always smiled at Reagan when she came in, and Peter's father liked to say logic puzzles to her and see if she could get the answer right by the next time she saw him. She only seriously tried to solve the puzzles one or two times, never actually solved one, but he kept throwing puzzles at her. She figured he missed having a girl in the house. She had never actually asked Peter if he was trans. The family photos in the hallway just shifted their focus smoothly and suspiciously from a girl baby wrapped in red rose blankets in the earliest photos to a shy-smiling girl child, an unsmiling girl teen, then jumped a couple of years to a leering husking boy with a dusting of mustache and terrible clothes, wattage dimmed on the smiles of the parents at his shoulders. He never talked about it.

I don't want candle wax on my shelves, he said. You shouldn't burn candles in the house. Candles are a hazard.

Candles are magic, said Reagan. Magic is the source of love. Love is the source of a good life. It's a total syllogism.

You don't know what you're doing, do you, said Peter.

I always know what I'm doing, said Reagan. Most people don't do that as well as me.

She stared into the flame of the black violet candle she'd set up on his pristine drafting table, cheap plastic leis of flowers from the party store downtown strewn around it. A book she'd read as a child told the story of a man who'd taught himself to see through objects by staring into the black space in a flame that the fire seemed to flow around like a rock in the river. She stared into the black space and tried not to see the fire burning around it.

I don't see what's so special about Josephine anyway, said Peter. What do you need her for? There are like a million other girls you could be with. Women are all the same anyway. They're like cars. You just go by color and style.

You're a misogynist piece of shit, said Reagan.

Oh, well, said Peter. You're a bad wizard.

He slumped on his pillows and started aggressively reading a yard-sale copy of Heavy Metal. From the kitchen the sizzle of greasy German meats, Peter's parents chattering quietly about the events of the day. Drawing Peter's parents was easy: sharp shovel jaws, clear blue eyes, a thin pen outline detailing shock-white hair. Reagan kept staring, ache building up behind her forehead.

§

Reagan and Josephine had worked it so that they got lockers together at the start of the year. Since it was far too late to reverse that, Josephine had proposed a system to Reagan. Josephine would get her books after second period and firth period; Josephine would get hers after third and sixth. Reagan usually ignored the system. The first thing her old social studies teacher had said you did when you invaded a country was you started to build infrastructure. That made it harder for the conquered peoples to resist or reject the invasion.

Josephine had the bottom locker, which gave Reagan the fifteen seconds it took to round the corner of the hallway and approach the lockers to admire her, crouched on her heels, her white peasant dress hanging off the curve of her back like the snow-covered edge of a cliff, the fringed hem a floating halo around her thin ankles.

Did you get my texts, she asked. Josephine blew angrily on her bangs and stood up, straightening her necklace of wooden beads carved like star signs.

I deleted your texts, she said. All my friends say it isn't good for us to talk right now.

Whoa, said Reagan. Defensive. I just asked you a question. I'm just getting my books for class.

We have a system, said Josephine. It would help me a lot if you'd follow the system.

I don't like the system, said Reagan. I like the idea of us back together.

No, Josephine said, and suddenly her face brightened. Hi Mike!

Josie, drawled Mike, an important classmate. His hair was gelled into spikes and he was already wearing a Harvard University sweater; he had gotten in early decision, everyone knew. Reagan watched him and remembered how she had looked at Josephine before, talking with Mike or other important classmates across the campus or the classroom, how she had turned back to her notebook paper and drawn cartoon girls sitting on unfurling leaves frowning at nothing. Fuck Mike, she thought.

How's my favorite artist? Mike asked.

Josephine threw her arms in the air, beaming welcome at him; he walked into them and patted her on the back. He looked at Reagan, who had gotten busy with opening her locker. Hi Reagan, he said. How's things?

Oh, can't complain, laughed Reagan. No one could possibly complain about anything! Nice sweater!

I earned it! Mike laughed, and Josephine did too.

The two of them started talking about a group project they were supposed to be finishing for history. Reagan listened to them, smiling a wide and dimpled smile, then opened her locker and took out the scissored up Harmon Metzger comic. She flipped the pages, letting Josephine see.

All right, I gotta bounce, said Mike. I'm going to go get hamburgers later, eat 'em by the duck pond. Interested?

Yeah maybe, said Josephine. Call me after fourth period.

Reagan yanked a page free of its staples as Mike walked away waving, and Josephine made a telephone gesture with her hands in reply. Then she turned furiously to Reagan.

Why are you reading Harmon Metzger, she demanded. Why are you tearing a Harmon Metzger comic up.

I'm allowed to read Harmon Metzger, smiled Reagan. I'm allowed to read whatever I want. You, however, are not allowed to eat by the duck pond. That's where you and I eat. That's where we met. It's illegal to eat there now.

I was eating at the duck pond first, said Josephine. It's mine. And you know that Harmon Metzger is my all-time favorite comics artist. Are you like, planning to read everything I read and wear the same clothes as me and become me? Is that what you're planning?

Reagan didn't answer. Josephine frowned and squinted, then reached forward and snatched the cut-up comic from Reagan's arms. She held the book by its spine and let it dangle down, the remaining strips of paper from the pages whose panels had been extracted dangling like snowflake mobiles.

Why did you cut it up? asked Josephine.

It's a secret, said Reagan. You'll find out. If you get back together with me maybe I won't have to cut up Harmon Metzger comic books any more.

Josephine stared at her. Reagan took the cut up book back, hoping Josephine would put up a fight and thus Reagan could touch her. Josephine didn't put up a fight. She blew out her bangs again and set her chin forward. She blinked, three times. She turned and walked away down the hall.

Reagan frowned and shoved the cut-up comic into her bag. Josephine was upset; so good; so let her think about what she'd done.

§

They had always eaten on the grass by the duck pond, Reagan putting her hand on Josephine's thigh where her skirt started in deliberate full view of the kids by the cafeteria's picture windows, then, rejected, throwing fried chicken bits to the ducks while Josephine told her to stop—that's *horrible* Reagan—invisible mites in the canyons of grass under their feet and hips devouring them. Now Reagan usually brought lunch from the gas station, which she ate while she wandered around by the air conditioning units on the far sides of the buildings, or she'd just sit and wait for her last period class to eat.

Her last period class was a study hall, designed for easy skipping. She spent it today in working on the secret Harmon Metzger project, cutting up panels.

Harmon Metzger liked to draw a lot of perverted stuff, all of it rendered in this goofy cartoon style, densely crosshatched in black; it all looked like Albrecht Durer doing Koko the Clown. Reagan had read a ton of it over Josephine's shoulders. Vividly she remembered doing that one night after her mother had broken a mug that had been important to her father, she guessed, and the kitchen had turned into a minefield and she had slipped down the street to Josephine's; she was trying to get Josephine to have sex with her so she could sleep, and Josephine had said she was busy, not in the mood, and she had kept on reading Harmon Metzger stories about women being tied up by malicious devils who then crawled into their snatches.

She had that story in front of her now. She was cutting out the best of these panels; she'd rearrange them into a new sequence, maybe white out the text and add her own, call the whole thing Meditations on the Death of Andrea Dworkin or something classy like that. Josephine had told her about Andrea Dworkin and how much she hated her and it would be a brilliant private joke between them to title it that. It was a shoo-in to go on the corkboard at the front of the room as long as she did something to censor the impolite stuff, nipples and pubic hair.

It was a beautiful plan. The thing about them is that both of them knew who Andrea Dworkin was; she knew Josephine missed this about her just as much as she missed it about Josephine. She had to. And Josephine would have to look at her classy art project every day: something she'd have loved to have done, something far beyond anything she could do for herself. Eventually this would lead to them getting back together and being in love for real. There was no better use for school than promoting love for real. The whole institution ought to be burned down to the extent that it failed to promote love for real. That was what her stupid peers could never understand, but Josephine might be made to.

She kept slicing up pages on the drafting table in her bedroom that Friday evening as soon as she got home, wondering where Josephine was, what friend she was seeing; she sliced through a human figure before her and threw the scraps away.

In a way it was a shame to cut up Metzger's pages; as reprehensible as the stuff he drew was, the way he drew it was flat-out beautiful: the tiny lines modeling hot pants; the deftly suggested ariolae bulging from breasts, even through the densest fabrics; the drips of sexual fluid oozing from overturned, architecturally splendid labias. Most people crosshatched with black lines at neat angles to one another, but Metzger's pen work was from Mars or something; some of it looked like weird spindly plants, others like spirals and pyramids, Norse runes that could have been physically gouged from the paper with a steel nib. Some of the marks even looked like letters. SECRET, these letters said.

Reagan frowned and squinted. The letters were so obscured in a maze of hatchwork that it was almost impossible to notice them, but once she had seen them she couldn't stop. SECRET.

The track shifted on the angry girl CD she was listening to on the art room's old player, and she only half heard a guitar riff she dearly loved.

She checked the panels before and after, scrutinizing them so hard her eyes started to water. There was nothing else she could find on that page, but there on the next was another, plain once you knew to look for it. GRAVITY, this one said.

She worked on, switching albums when she had to. By eight she had found everything there was to find. After another half hour she figured she had put all the words in the right order.

SHOE CLOSET OF DEATH HOUSE HAS SECRET. BLACK GRAVITY SWALLOWS EVERYTHING.

3

There was only one comic book store in Austin that stayed open past nine o'clock. She walked out of the school building. Night school students—dropouts, people with day jobs, ex-prisoners, the ambitious homeless—walked toward her in a column, and she jostled them aside and unlocked her bike, shivering. There had been a rain that afternoon and the asphalt was wet, the tires of her bike wobbling in the long grooves generations of sanitation trucks had sliced into the bike lane.

I need every comic book you sell by Harmon Metzger, she said to the old man behind the counter of the store. He straightened up to his full height, six five, and hitched up his jeans to expand to his full width, three two, the R. Crumb doodle on his black T-shirt spreading like a sail. He itched the place where his silver braided goatee stretched the flesh of his chin.

You know Harmon Metzger? he asked. You're into him? You have this?

He pulled the issue of PHUCKBOOK PHUNNIES she already had off of the Recommended Reading rack by the cash box.

I've read that one, yeah, she said. Do you have anything else by him?

That's it, he said. Shit, I wish I had a different answer for you. People don't like his stuff much anymore. You can go to jail sometimes for selling his stuff.

I won't rat you out, Reagan said. Can you maybe order some of the jailbait stuff for me? I'll pay in advance.

Who are you, you beautiful apparition? asked the owner. Pretty girl all asking to read more of that sad old fucker's work. Harmon would've loved you. You're exactly his physical type, even. That real solid dykey look to you.

I am a dyke, yes, Reagan said.

I'm sorry for using that word, he said.

It's fine, smiled Reagan. You should give me a discount on my order, though. For reparations.

The owner pointed with a massive, sweat-logged arm to a drawing of a writhing naked woman who looked kind of like Josephine looked in Reagan's dreams, only impaled on a trident in the hands of a devil with an unambiguously phallic nose. WANT A DISCOUNT? chuckled the devil. NOT A CHANCE IN HELL!

Harmon did that for me, he beamed.

It's the most beautiful thing I've yet seen, said Reagan. So you knew Harmon Metzger?

For like ten years, said the owner happily. Asshole lived here, in Austin, until he bit the dust. Used to hang out in the back room here and draw and knock back a few. Said he didn't like to be alone so much when he drank and drew.

He's dead? asked Reagan. How did he die?

The owner's face went blank; the goatee dropped, slack, like a rope. The bell rang as some customers came in.

He hung himself, said the owner. That's the short answer.

Oh God, said Reagan. Sorry.

You didn't do it, said the owner.

She stood by the counter and waited, female voices slurring drunkenly from somewhere in the manga racks.

It's fine, continued the owner. I don't mind talking about it, getting over it. I mean I was there and everything. You ever been out by Lava Caves Road?

That's the best name for a road, Reagan said. No, I haven't.

He used to live out there, said the owner. This crazy Spanish shack out there. We were watching Modern Times, this nuts old Chaplin movie where Chaplin does cocaine and fights robots and just all kinds of things. Harmon loved that stuff; he kind of made you love it, to know him. It just finished and he was whistling the song that plays at the end. He was a hell of a whistler. I bet you'd like to be walking down the highway forever with Paulette Goddard, I said to him. Yeah, he said. It's a beautiful world they live in, beautiful black and white world. I've got to use the bathroom. I told him, Don't fall in. I can't believe that's the last thing I ever said to him.

He lived in Austin? Reagan asked. Is that house still here?

Yeah, it's still there, out by the airport, said the owner. It looks so bad I still notice it when I'm taking a plane somewhere. It spoils my whole plane ride. No one lives there now. He had this will all ready to go when he pulled the rope. It was all hand-lettered too, crosshatched around the border. I don't know what his deal was with that crosshatch stuff. One of the clauses is that the house was to lie fallow—I think that's how he put it, lie fallow—for ten years. So no one's there. There's an overseer who's supposed to go out and look after it from time to time, but the guy moved away a year ago. The place is probably completely fucked up with rats and squatters by now.

He didn't have a wife, or kids, or anything? asked Reagan.

Harmon had kind of a problem with women, said the owner. I don't know if that surprises you.

No, Reagan said.

Maybe a wife would've been good for him, said the owner. Maybe he'd have lived longer and drawn less completely horrible illegal stuff. I don't know. Twenty-twenty, that's hindsight.

Why didn't anyone contest this will? asked Reagan. When someone's crazy, you can contest the will and get it made invalid. That fallow thing is pretty nuts. So is hanging yourself after watching a Charlie Chaplin movie.

The owner tapped a pen against the counter.

The only reason you'd contest a will is to get someone's things, he said. What would you end up with if you contested Harmon's will? The deed to that fucked up house? The rights to a bunch of books it's basically treasonous to print?

I guess that makes sense, Reagan said.

Course it makes sense, said the owner. Who wants to end up like Harmon Metzger?

§

It was forty minutes to close; she trawled the back racks of the store anyway. Some new company was publishing Uncle Scrooge back issues and she paged through a big anthology. It had a story she'd never read before in it. She squinted at the pages and then put it away. It seemed abstract, irrelevant somehow for Uncle Scrooge to have new adventures.

Reagan! called a voice. She turned; it was Miss Stevens. She was wearing a zebra-print skirt that showed off her knees more than Reagan had ever seen in the classroom. A tall woman was with her wearing a soft burgundy sweater, sensible jeans, a wide smile. Miss Stevens approached, stumbling.

Carol, this is Reagan, one of my students, said Miss Stevens. Reagan, this is Carol, my partner.

It's lovely to meet you, said Carol, bending her knees slightly to offer a cold hand. I've heard so much about you.

Good things, laughed Miss Stevens.

Oh good, said Reagan.

There was a terrible silence; she breathed in the gin on her teacher's breath.

So, said Miss Stevens. Is this one of your hangouts, Reagan?

Hangouts, laughed Reagan. Why do you ask? Do you come here a lot?

We're just here getting our manga fix, smiled Miss Stevens.

She showed Reagan the cover of one of the tiny manga volumes she held in her hands. The cover showed a bat-winged devil girl and a white-winged angel girl hovering over either shoulder of a schoolgirl who stood over a gigantic bowl of ice cream and bananas, her hair tall and pink, her eyes confused and tempted and sad. There was a huge chunk of the ice cream missing, and the girl's face was colored green, like she was feeling sick. A cherubic rat with a mysterious kanji character hovering over his head was dancing in the foreground.

This is one of our favorite series, Miss Stevens said.

The artwork is rilly good, said Carol, eyes twinkling.

Oh, it is, said Miss Stevens. Oh, Reagan, let me give this to you, actually. You should study the line work. It's clean and elegant but still detailed and evocative. It's really good to make practice copies from.

Yeah, said Reagan. I'd love to read about that girl who eats a lot of cake. Definitely.

Miss Stevens beamed and gave her the book, maybe forgetting she hadn't yet paid for it. Reagan slipped it into her shopping bag and waved to the owner of the store on the way out; he waved back and flipped the page of PHUCKBOOK FUNNIES over the cover, biting his lip.

§

In her bed, she sent Josephine a text message: *Do you like mysteries?? Well does ol Reagan have a mystery for YOU. It's about your favorite artist. Skip school with me tomorrow and we'll go solve it together. It will be our first date in the new world order. You can not say no to me.*

She sat working on arranging the panels she'd cut out into the order of the message on a piece of Bristol board for two hours, the phone by her side. She checked the phone one last time before going to bed. No reply. She put the phone in her desk drawer, closed it, taped up the edges. After lying in bed for a half hour she got up, cut the tape, went to sleep with the phone in her hands.

4

She skipped school Wednesday and checked the phone book at a 7-11. Harmon Metzger was still listed on Lava Caves Road. Still no reply from Josephine. Fuck that bitch; Reagan'd solve the mystery alone.

She walked down Lamar to the park by the river where the economics students wore shorts and played frisbee golf. She sat on the limestone banks of the creek and studied the linework of the manga volume. On page after page, clean-lined representations of angel and devil girls ate cake, swooned, exploded in rage with blood bursting from their noses and fire from their mouths.

She imagined Miss Stevens and Carol sitting on their bed, floral spread, a pile of these comics between them. They would each read a volume, laugh, point out panels to one another, trade. Maybe one or the other of them would dress up like the characters, wear brilliant Day-Glo wigs. They would fall asleep in each other's arms. Soft flower petals and hearts would rise from the space between them. Reagan closed her eyes and lay back against the rock and ached with the thought of it.

§

The first bus in the chain of buses required to get out to Lava Caves Road had two stops, equally distant from Reagan; she took the stop outside Josephine's house. She sat on the bench the next weekend with her sketchbook and pen ready and watched in Josephine's window. Josephine was at school, but Reagan looked anyway on the off chance she had been sick or something. She'd seen Josephine smoking pot in the window once. Today she saw nothing. She sketched Josephine's house anyway: sharp vertical lines, converging as they went up, as if she was an ant at its feet. She tried to use clean lines, romantic manga lines, lots of white space and thick cartoon contours.

§

From online maps she knew how far away Harmon Metzger's house was supposed to be, but on Capital Metro buses it seemed to take far longer. The bus was stuffed with people en route to clearly terrible jobs, people who had to take this bus every day, and among them were people who had obviously never held jobs, could never hold jobs, could never want jobs or understand what jobs could do for you. There were kids visiting friends, eyes vacant and locked on smartphone games; there were whole families sitting too stoically, Reagan thought, for a weekend; the families sat across multiple seats with strollers, diaper bags, fanny packs, an ancient Polaroid camera around patriarchal necks—*we're gonna have fun today kids, right kids, right kids,* the mother was saying—and Lava Caves Road was in the extreme south of town; there was nothing beyond it; where could this family possibly be going that would be so fun; maybe they would take the bus all the way to the end of the line, get out and take photos next to the terminal sign, alone on a deserted road, then they would turn around and get back on the bus going in the other direction, get back to where they'd started and snap photos of their neighborhood, get to bed early so they could get up for work in the morning, on evenings invite friends over to see photo slides of the terminus and the front of their own house; *maybe riding the bus had become their entire lives.*

At every stop, it seemed, there was a panhandler, leather-skinned and wearing kerchiefs, olive drab caps, aviators; they all approached the door with folding cardboard signs, crumpled pieces of paper, backs of books, all bearing desperate messages in Sharpie and sweat stains in the shape of fingers and palms. They stopped a good three feet from the door and waited politely for the people getting off to come to them. Reagan tried not to make eye contact with them.

It was a mile walk from the bus stop to Harmon Metzger's death house, a walk where the sidewalk kept disappearing and the shoulder of the road flexed from a full and generous line to mere molecules of asphalt where the yellow department of transportation road paint had missed or had faded away from age and never been replaced, and then the sidewalk was gone and Reagan found herself in crushed-down grass strewn with Coke bottles and supermarket bags of junk food wrappers and household trash as giant cars tore past her right shoulder at eighty miles per hour and airplanes tore up the sky to her left, taking off and landing from the airport that squatted like an anthill at the edge of long fields.

Eventually the desolation tapered off into a micro-suburb, maybe three streets crossing in either direction like a lizard's tail torn from the body of the main city and still whipping around on the echo of a missing nervous system. She found Metzger's house easily. The man at the comic shop had not been wrong; the place looked as if it had started as a kind of Spanish-style shack from the 1950s and then been subject to a series of Dr. Mengele home improvements, modifications, additions, avocado-and-magenta paint jobs. Layers of clashing paint showed through one another in a kind of nauseating, aspirational vitiligo. The yard hadn't been touched since Metzger's suicide, or so it looked, and the mixture of bermuda grass, dandelions, fire ant mounds, and fallen branches that made up the landscaping scraped the bottom of the windowsills and shook in unison when wind shot from jet engines across the fields.

It was easy to break into this terrible place. Whole sections of fence were missing, and the back door didn't even have a lock. Other people had figured this out long before Reagan: ancient sleeping bags lay abandoned on the carpet, and beer bottles and microwave dinner packaging stained the coffee table, sat empty on the shelves, lay in the corners where boots had kicked them. A kid had spraypainted something difficult to make out across one full wall of the kitchen: OBAMA NUKES, or something like it, was the icing that topped dozens of woven graffiti tags on the same wall like the history of a dead empire gouged into stone tablets. Behind the graffiti there were fields of whiter spaces against the cigarette-yellow cast of the walls' original paint job, holes drilled into sheet rock and wall studs in those white fields, evidence that something had hung on these walls—paintings? drawings? photographs?—something that someone had taken away forever.

And yet beyond the main room, where the squatters had spent their time, the place was eerily immaculate, orderly like the bedroom of a troubled child. Different rooms boasted rows of toy soldiers, robots, Russian dolls with their jewel-eyes glittering from the shelves. Stacks of paperback books covered every other surface—cheap sci-fi, doomsday prophecies, Jungian pop-psych, histories of cults, the odd nineteenth century American classic in dirt cheap reprint edition—all the books trued at the edges and covered in dust. A Felix the Cat clock ticked on the wall, one of its shifty eyes put out and the tail no longer connected to the inner workings of the clock but hanging loosely from wires, lashing back and forth like the end of a knotted rope as the clock gears advanced. She moved through the space, not wanting to breathe: despite the strange order of the room, the never-filtered air felt thick with accumulated grime, with dessicated parts of roaches and spiders. If she breathed these would come in, reassemble inside her.

She looked in the bathroom where according to the owner of the comic shop Metzger had done it. The bathroom was the cleanest part of the house, the baseboards scrubbed and the mirror spotless despite the dust, sparkling in what sun came through the red curtains. Reagan opened the curtains the rest of the way; the dull steel bar above the shower glowed like foundry metal. She put her finger on the bar and traced its faint curve back to the wall. There was a hairline crack in the paint where the bar joined the sheet rock; she could look into the dark hole formed and see crumbs of plaster, the beginnings of webs. She rested her finger on the crack and felt a needle of wind on the ridges of her finger, some secret conduit of air that ran through these walls from the world outside.

There was no desk or drafting table or any evidence of where Metzger might have worked. The round kitchen table, on second inspection, was scarred with knife marks, and all the chairs were missing.

She found the bedroom easily: a low mattress on a black metal frame, a blanket with lighthouses stretched over it, neatly tucked and folded. There was a squat Danish nightstand with a paperback on it, some publication by a cult that related to time travel, a page folded back to mark a place. She sat on Metzger's bed and opened the book. Whole paragraphs had not just been crossed out but cross-hatched out, as if great black spiders had nested on the page. The crosshatching made her eyes burn, and she put the book down and took a long breath. She could feel the dust making room for her.

She stretched out on the suicide's bed and closed her eyes.

Outside the tangle of lawn was moving, and a sluggish ice cream truck played Turkey in the Straw, its melody oozing between the houses. She felt the dust in the air shift and the long-calcified sweat of the suicide's covers start to melt and coat her skin, and she imagined the suicide was in the room with her, the toilet just flushed and water still restoring itself, his slow shuffle back to the window, grumble of curses, Venetian blinds opening and shutting, his hands putting a record on the weary portable player on the shelf. She imagined him though she knew nothing about Harmon Metzger: his career, his childhood, why he had evidently never found a wife or found anyone at all in the world, where he went when he left his house and got in his car and drove to be driving somewhere, anywhere else, whether he had masturbated in this bed, what he had thought about if he had, what songs could make him cry, how he had felt as the initial blush of fame, or just monetary success, or just the ability to pay basic bills and food costs, basic self-sufficiency, how he had felt as these things had fled him, what it had felt like to him to make the vases-into-profiles shift from being young with success just around the corner to being old and failed—she knew nothing about him, only knew that lying in his bed and listening to the weeds and dogs of Lava Caves road howl felt good to her. She felt for the first time that she had never really been to sleep before, only closed her eyes and went away, and now the quickening sweat of the room held her tight like a blanket, and it was like a trap door had opened at the bottom of the sleep she had known about before and she descended through it like she was riding on the roof of a rusty ancient elevator, gently swaying on its counterweight, into a deeper, richer cavern of sleep, where if she shouted to the unseen walls of her new unconsciousness it might take years for the echo to come back.

§

She woke up; the sun was nearly down and the bedroom was already blue and dark. She got out of bed, head aching, and went to the closet. The bottom shelf was a row of nearly identical brown boat shoes with one pair of huaraches, the sole perforated by a nail. Behind the sandals she found a black bag with white machine-printed letters: ESPN DEPORTES. The bag was heavy and something cold was inside. To touch it felt like she was handling ice through an oven mitt. She unzipped the bag; it was full of paper towels. She took out a wad of towels and peeled them free of the heavy thing they protected. A vast oval gemstone, the diameter of a salad plate, flattened out on the top and bottom and myriad facets askew to one another along the outer rims. It was an emerald, so green it was black.

She set it on the ground in front of her and stared, breathing heavily, at this thing she had discovered.

Something was moving inside the black emerald. She looked closer, but no, nothing was moving, was it: it had almost been a black tendril, a string of ink dissolving in water, but maybe it had only been the last movement of the setting sun.

She put the emerald in her backpack and left the death house, walked into the back yard and closed the lockless door behind her. The evening wind had increased as the Monday overseas commuters took off on their night flights to Europe or Singapore or wherever and the tangled mass of lawn was wrenching from side to side from the suck of the engines that cried overhead. It was just a matter of finding the path she'd made in the lawn when she'd come in a lifetime ago, and then a matter of sitting at the bus stop along Lava Caves Road for an hour and twenty minutes before the night bus rolled in late from the terminus, its seats empty but for a shaking old woman, the driver playing Mingus album cuts on an out-of-date tape deck and refusing to give Reagan change for the ride back uptown.

5

A sedately abstract German board game sat between Peter, his father, his mother, a tray of nuts and raisins beside each player. Reagan made sure to slam the screen door to let them know she was there.

Ah, Reagan, said Peter's father, his eyes lighting up. The daughter I never had.

Would you like some dinner? Peter's mother said. Would you care to make a fourth? The game's far more strategically dense with four people.

I'll bet it is, said Reagan. Can I steal Peter? We have to solve a mystery together.

You can hardly steal him, said Peter's mother, smiling sadly, when he is freely given to you.

§

There's no way to test if it's an emerald, said Peter, in the bedroom. Based on the weight it could go either way. You'd have to like drop it off at a lab.

Do you know any such labs? Reagan asked.

Maybe at the university, said Peter. Actually, I wouldn't drop it off at a lab. If it is an emerald it's got to be like the most valuable emerald ever. If I were some kid researcher working at a lab I'd totally jack that emerald. I'd sell it and buy, like, a nuclear submarine, work as a privateer. Live free off the government black ops dime. Aw yeah. You want to sell it to me?

No, said Reagan. If it's that valuable I'm keeping it.

It's not valuable unless you have a buyer, said Peter. That's how economics works.

It's valuable to me, Reagan said.

Maybe you're just afraid of changing your situation, Peter said.

I'm not afraid to change my situation, she said. Josephine's not my girlfriend anymore. I'm changing that situation.

Peter grunted again, lying on his bed, the copy of PHUCKBOOK PHUNNIES tented over his eyes. Reagan sat at the drafting table in the corner of the room, the walls as eerily bare as those in her own bedroom, nothing to look at but the tunnel a pushpin had made to hold some long-since-removed poster. The manga book Miss Stevens and her partner had given her lay cracked open on the drafting table. Reagan had been practicing, copying drawings of maids and impeccable classrooms and chibi creatures. Now she was working on a new drawing that incorporated the style: those bright wet eyes, weird steel lakes, the frozen emotion in the tiny mouths, a shorthand of feelings. She worked dutifully, took each device and tinkered with it and laid it out on the page. She stopped and looked down.

Oh shit, Peter, she said. Shit, come look at this. I drew Josephine.

So what? he said. You draw Josephine all the time. Hey—does this look familiar?

No, this looks familiar, she said. I drew a manga Josephine. Without even trying to. That's fucked. I'm totally obviously in love. If you draw someone without even trying to you're totally obviously in love.

You're so full of platitudes, Peter said. Seriously, look at this thing in this panel.

You're so full of shit, Reagan said.

She admired her drawing, the bowl cut feathered by fading pen marks, the spiral ear piercing so illegal by dress code standards but nobody upheld these, the goofy raver necklace nestled in the valley of her outsize hoodie's collar, those wet-steel eyes locked in place. She added fantasy-size breasts and a network of clothing folds that highlighted the same; she carved away at the jawline. She had just finished this when Peter set the copy of PHUCKBOOK PHUNNIES on the drawing board over her work. She tried to stab his hand with her pen.

Look, Peter said, deflecting the nib.

For some reason Harmon Metzger had taken it upon himself to draw a slapstick torture chamber in the background of a densely hatched page-wide panel. In the context of any other comic book it might have been a standout, kind of a virtuoso tour of sociopath's whimsy; in the context of Metzger's work it was pretty par. The girls cavorted, lashed one another with black whips, kicked ribs of the omega males who sprawled around the deftly suggested grime of the floor, heated pokers and cackled with the hot metal casting black shadows behind their cheeks, broke thumbs in screws of men on Catherine wheels. And in the background, wearing a fantastical headdress of teal feathers, silver sequins, tafetta grasses, a monstrous bird queen dreamed, fat coins weighing down her eyelids. You could almost have missed her in the crosshatching. The black emerald sat between her breasts. You'd know it anywhere. Paradoxical teeth were exposed between the halves of the bird queen's beak; she looked in pain or in ecstasy or in both.

Reagan set the comic book down in her lap.

I never would've seen that in a million years, she said. How did you notice that?

I was looking for secret messages, he said. Obviously if he included one he'd include more.

I already checked for secret messages, she said. There weren't any.

You didn't know this was a secret message before you figured out what the first secret message was about, Peter said. It's hella cunning.

She stared through the veil of ink at the dreaming bird queen's face, the gap in her sighing teeth.

Do you think it matters what kind of coins you use? she asked. He just drew little cent signs on these. Do you think it has to be pennies? I have two quarters but not any pennies.

She dug for the quarters in her jeans pockets while Peter started, the reflex jounce of his knee sending anxious vibrations through the mattress.

You have to let me stay the night, also, she said. You don't mind the futon, right? I would take the futon, but she's on a bed in the picture and I want to get it as close as possible.

What are you talking about, Peter said, and stood up. I don't understand the basic point of the things you're saying. It's as if you're just shrieking like an animal.

I mean think about it, Reagan said. Before, I found a secret message hidden in this guy's drawings, right? And it was all like, directions to find a ginormous emerald. Now we find another secret message, and it's all instructions for a weird ritual using the emerald. We have to figure out this second message, don't we?

Maybe it's just a prop, Peter said. Just a cool, fantastically expensive thing that he liked to draw, like one of those wooden model men with the bubble heads, only made out of platinum. Maybe he used it as like a doorstop in another comic that we don't have.

Then we'll find out that it's just a cool thing he liked to draw, she said.

She lay back on Peter's bed, closed her eyes, set the quarters over her eyelids. It only took a few seconds before they ached; she tried to let her eyes flutter open and they wouldn't respond.

Reagan, said Peter; she shifted.

I can't tell where you are, she said. Did you move? Are you getting the emerald? Here.

She pulled up her shirt to the collarbone, wriggling to do it but keeping the quarters level.

Reagan, Peter said again after a moment. Um, like in the drawing they're doing this ritual in a torture chamber. Does that not bother you?

The part of the drawing about the emerald probably doesn't have anything to do with the rest of the drawing, she said.

Why would you assume that? he asked.

Besides, what's torturous about drawings? she continued, ignoring him. —A drawing can't torture you.

What if you go to sleep with that thing on your, your chest, Peter said, and when you wake up you're like in Hell? Or in a glass cylinder in some kind of lab on the other side of a dimensional gateway, your neck and sides all hooked up to tubes, and they're sucking the lymph out of you, because it's like gold to them? Like lymph is the scarcest substance in their dimension? Which explains why they let the emerald go.

Don't describe your fantasy life to me, she said. Just lay this fucking emerald on my chest.

She listened; his feet scruffed the carpet, went away from her a moment—he was getting the emerald—came back toward her, louder—he was standing over her. And the cold weight was pressing down on her chest. Its surface tension sucked up the sweat of her skin; a puff of hot breath forced its way out of her nose, her lips.

It's heavier than I thought, she said.

He didn't say anything; she tried to adjust her breathing to the weight of the thing. The difficulty in breathing made her panic, and she tried to adjust her mind to the panic as well.

Peter, she said.

What's our plan? Peter asked. I mean, if you're pulled into an evil dimension? Should I try to come after you? Or should I just like, learn how to write stories, and then write your story, and tell everyone we know about what became of you?

Jesus, said Reagan. I'm going to go to sleep for a while, and probably I'm going to cough a lot, and in the morning we'll crack up about how we thought we were going to find some kind of cool secret message in a dirty comic book, and we'll eat parent leftovers for breakfast.

Long silence.

Peter? she asked.

Do you have to sleep on the bed? Peter asked. I hate the futon. You actually like the futon.

Don't be a total dick, Reagan said.

§

They kept talking, on and off, the spaces between words getting longer and longer as Reagan fell into strange alpha patterns of thought and Peter flipped through different comic anthologies on the shelves. At some point Reagan realized—from what sense she still had of the light that crept into her eyes around the cracks between coins and eyelids—that the light had been out for a while. Peter was murmuring in sleep from somewhere, from the floor? She could feel nothing around her but the waft of dryer sheet from the covers and the weight of metal and gemstone on her eyes and chest.

Peter? she asked.

There was a murmur from somewhere in the blackness. Was it Peter? Was the room still here? The bed still felt the same, but that meant nothing. She could be anywhere. She could be floating through an infinite void, only the mattress holding her up and the emerald holding her from lifting off in the gravity vacuum. She could be under glass in a lush jungle with the flowers breathing sleep poisons at her. She could be in a castle stocked with devils and goblins, with bird queens who sharpened knives to carve her liver out and devour it, shrieks rising into the night.

Peter, she called again, and tried to breathe slowly.

Beneath the metallic spice of the quarters she could smell dryer sheets cooking with the yet-to-be-folded clothes. She breathed it in, slow, out, slow.

§

It was hard to get to sleep again, on her back as she was with her eyes held shut like a mummy. If only the sensory deprivation were more complete it might be easier, but now that she could smell the dryer sheet smell she couldn't stop noticing it, and now it was accompanied by the strange mechanical sounds in the walls and Peter's body shifting, and through the crack in the window cold leaves and moving air, the taste of trapped breath and plaque in her mouth. All this plus the weight of the emerald—its heat, now, all drawn from her body and made its own—combined into a single scratchy sense, one that painted itself across the black canvas of her vision, a million luminous iron filings moving as though some maniac was crossing a magnet over them like a conductor's baton, an animate sand painting in metal.

The synesthetic picture formed.

Reagan and Josephine, walking arm in arm down a path in an windblown forest, dust clouds kicking from their bare toes, Reagan talking, dusty luna moths spiraling out of her dancing mouth, brilliant on every subject; she was saying all the right things at all the right moments at last, and Josephine utterly charmed, utterly silent. A question; agreement; another question; agreement. Josephine smiled, beautiful, complacent, silent.

No, this was not right; the picture quivered and adjusted: as Josephine spoke, archers behind her teeth fired arrows; each pierced the heart of the moths still spiraling from Reagan's mouth, sent them to the ground between the two where they vanished in pixelated sprays. The two stopped moving. The wind blew scattering pinwheels from the trees along the path, defoliated them completely, until all hue was gone and there was only white light and emptiness in alternating bands. Reagan waited; Josephine waited; neither spoke.

Her heart beneath the emerald's weight surged, yearned; the picture quivered and adjusted again; Josephine burst into song, eyes insane; arrows and bombs and disasters arced from her throat and began to shatter the silhouette profile of Reagan's face. She felt the emerald weigh on her and told her strange avatar endure it, endure it, only don't let her stop speaking, and every minute her avatar grew smaller, miniature, microscopic, and the emerald grew heavier and heavier against her sternum, its weight forcing the lock of her rib cage open, and the flood from Josephine's mouth was about to sweep away all that was Reagan along with the windy edges of the trees, everything gone.

And at last her self in all its diabolical and ugly glory appeared in fire; she saw it and she loved it and she did not want it to disappear.

Pounds of snow fell into the picture and covered every black metal line in soft white.

The ground as the snow melted and ran off lost its nauseous brightness, was brown and gray and white as it ought to be; everything had become extremely clear.

§

The light hurt when Peter took the coins off her eyelids and they flipped up of their own accord; she winced and rolled on her side and felt the emerald thud off of her and onto the mattress. She pulled the covers over her chest.

What happened? asked Peter. Are you in an evil dimension now? Is this the real Reagan? When is my birthday, if this is the real Reagan?

Did your parents leave us coffee, Reagan groaned. Did you check.

Tell me what happened, said Peter, crawling up next to her on the bed and folding his legs under himself. He took the black emerald between his hands, hefted it.

Nothing happened, said Reagan. I had a bad dream, is all.

What was bad about it? asked Peter.

Nothing, said Reagan. I don't know. Can I have a shirt?

Peter brought her one and then excused himself. She lay on the bed as soon as his door closed, groaning as the hours of coin pressure on the orbital bones of her eye sockets were slowly released as headache. She got up and put the shirt on. She cruised the rows of Peter's books, DVDs, the papers on his desk.

She was still looking at the desk when Peter came back with two steins of coffee and a plate of bratwurst and eggs, singing the little melody that played in Zelda when you found an important item.

Duh-nuh-nuh-nuhhhh, he sang. We live another day.

He and the smell of the food came up behind her, his voice next to her ear. The black expanse on the page, a thick empty black crust of ink over the smooth white paper, like the shell of a dead thing from the sea.

Neat drawing, Peter said. Did you do that last night?

This isn't what I drew at all, said Reagan.

6

The drawing, hanging at the front of the art classroom: The light of the flat screen monitor at the bottom left corner of the image broke the purity of Josephine's face into tiny slash marks of pen hatching, thin where they began like the halos in medieval paintings of queens, then thickening as they raked backward across Josephine's cheeks, weaving a dense blackness that sculpted the back half of her head like a nun's cowl made of pitch, an ink spider she wore like a crown. Her hair floated over it like feathers and you could feel the weight of each feather, the tumbling imbalance of vane and rachis; you could feel them moving against the suck of the air conditioning intake. Her skull had a weight too, a papal orb lazily entrusted to her altar of upturned palms, elbows resting on the desk. A pile of books beside her elbows, the letters of the titles suggested rather than spelled out, but certainly items essential in the library of a frail literary teen: your Brontës, your *Eyre*, your Safran Foer, your Plath and your Tom Robbins and your *Flowers in the Attic*. Beside the books, a DVD of *The Royal Tenenbaums*. Beside the DVD, a dish of chicken and spinach, a fork, no doubt brought up from a mother's loving oven, family dinner skipped, promising daughter needed to study. The dinner was half-eaten. The books were untouched. Lines of language snaked from the edge of the flatscreen, lyrics to an autotuned ballad, a woman wronged and alone and surviving, text blending skillfully with the crosshatch background, suggestions of posters gleaming through the linework, the pop idol who sang the ballad crouching in a tight vinyl dress in front of a graffiti on brick set dressing, fog machines belching into a 1980s alleyway of urban dreams. Josephine's eyes were cartoons, holes into her face into which your emotions fell, mingled with the feelings the Artist had put there: strange sadness, refusal to admit that sadness, touch of boredom, touch of being willingly hypnotized. A word bubble snaked over her head: I AM A YOUNG WOMAN OF SUBSTANCE. The lines filled the paper, choked out the white space with black.

What do we think of this, Miss Stevens asked. Anyone?

The only anyone who mattered didn't raise her hand. Reagan stared into her back, tried to burn the nerves in her shoulder blades, force her arms up.

After a few more moments of silence another hand went up.

Michael, said Miss Stevens.

The assignment was to do a collage, said Michael. This isn't a response to the assignment.

Miss Stevens smiled.

Sometimes art is about breaking the rules, she said. What if the artist is playing with the notions of a collage, Michael? By presenting the work in the context of this assignment? Don't you think? Can a collage not maybe be a collage of paper, and ink, and white space?

Isn't everything potentially a collage, then? asked another student. Am I a collage, of like flesh and clothes and ideas? Can I turn myself in?

These are interesting questions, said Miss Stevens. Does anyone have anything that maybe responds more directly to this work?

I think it's mean, said a girl. I think it's incredibly mean and conceited to think of someone this way.

Reagan, her arms hanging at her sides, clenched her pencil and fought the urge to raise it; you couldn't speak during your own critique. This was an iron rule. She thought instead: you know nothing. It isn't mean; it's true. She squinted and tried to turn her thoughts into a drill that bored into the skull of this bitch. It isn't mean it's true. It isn't mean it's true.

The class went on discussing the girl in the picture, different interpretations of her. She was a woman of substance; the books indicated this. The lyrics of the song she was listening to had substance. Lyrics were really like poetry, the poems of today. If Shakespeare or Milton or someone was alive today he would probably be a rock lyricist. He and Mozart could have a band. The woman in the picture was fine. Really there was nothing wrong with her. The artist had failed in her work. The picture was a celebration.

Five minutes before the bell Josephine said she had to go to the bathroom. She took her bag with her. Reagan watched her disappear out the door without turning her head to the critique corkboard.

When the bell rang some of the students came up to Reagan to apologize. It wasn't her they thought was mean, the students explained. It was the piece. They wanted her to know this. She said she understood and said she had to hurry to her locker. But Miss Stevens was waiting by the door. The picture had been taken down from the corkboard; she held it at one corner by the tips of her fingers, like it was covered in something.

Reagan, she smiled, tightly. Please come to my office a minute.

One had no choice when a teacher said this. One went with her into her office just at the corner of the room, again the orange stool, the psychedelic blanket, the ficus, which was thriving.

So, said Miss Stevens. Your new piece. Let's talk about it.

What about it? asked Reagan. What people said today?

I'm sorry about that, said Miss Stevens. People normally shouldn't make those kind of personal attacks.

Reagan shrugged.

The drawing isn't mean, she said. It's true.

Miss Stevens looked at her.

The drawing was quite outstanding, she said. Very, very good. By far the best piece I've seen you turn in.

Thanks, said Reagan. I, um, I guessed you thought that, since you put it on the board and all.

I did, said Miss Stevens. I wanted to let you have that experience.

She paused, looked at the carpet.

There's not an easy way to ask this, she said. Is that drawing entirely yours?

Reagan stared at Miss Stevens' eyes, suddenly level with her own; against the back of her skull she could feel the black emerald, the heat of its projection.

You mean, did I draw it, she asked.

I need to know if this is your own work, Miss Stevens said. Out of fairness to the other students. Do you understand?

Reagan stared at the floor.

You think I wasn't capable of doing this? she asked.

I think you're capable of anything, said Miss Stevens. You and anyone else in this school. But this is—something very much beyond what you've previously done. Something suspiciously beyond what you've previously done, Reagan.

The emerald's weight in her brain; the memory of the emerald's weight on her chest.

It's a picture of Josephine, she said finally, to the carpet. How could it not have come from me, if it's a picture of Josephine?

This is Josephine? asked Miss Stevens. Reagan looked up; she was frowning at the picture.

Of course it's Josephine, said Reagan. It looks just like her.

I can see it now, Miss Stevens said slowly. I see, yes. It's Josephine.

You're our art teacher, said Reagan. How do you not know what Josephine looks like? Everyone else in the class got it.

Miss Stevens sat further back in her chair and picked up a Sailor Scout mug of tea.

It's a very beautifully done picture, she said. Of Josephine. I worry about this picture of Josephine. I maybe would not have put this picture up, had I known this was a picture of Josephine.

Why not? asked Reagan.

She slid off the stool and bounced on her toes against the carpet, propped herself back up, nervous habit; Miss Stevens watched her slide up and down.

Reagan, she asked. You and Josephine were very close, as people, weren't you?

We were dating, yeah, said Reagan. We will be again.

Miss Stevens was watching her, eyes tight.

We can't not be dating, said Reagan. It's essentially against God.

Do you feel alone without Josephine? Miss Stevens asked.

Reagan frowned.

As a queer teenager, Miss Stevens said, if that's how you identify, of course. I don't mean to assume anything. But as a queer teenager. Did she make you feel less alone?

Reagan blinked again and looked at the carpet. She felt bad

for Miss Stevens all of a sudden.

I identify as queer, personally, continued Miss Stevens. Just so that you know. I don't want you to think that I use that word pejoratively, if it makes you uncomfortable.

I know you identify as queer, said Reagan, sharply. I met your girlfriend, remember?

Miss Stevens sat back, picked up her tea again, sucked at the rim of the glass.

Are you doing okay at home, Reagan? she asked finally. Family supportive of you? No problems?

What's that supposed to mean? asked Reagan. I have the perfect family. They leave me alone.

Okay, said Miss Stevens. And you feel personally okay. School isn't too much pressure? Maybe it's not challenging you enough?

I feel fine, said Reagan, flatly.

Miss Stevens nodded, chewed a nail, watched her.

I'm going to write you a hall pass, she said. It's good for whenever you want it, my class or any other class. If you ever feel, you know—stressed. Hurt. Isolated. Like you just want to talk. Please use it.

She wrote out the pass and handed it to Reagan. It was to the school counselor's office.

Please don't think this says anything negative about you, said Miss Stevens, then tried to smile. Reagan watched her smile, this woman who was trying to help her.

Are you going to put my drawing back up on the cork board, she asked.

I think that would be questionable, said Miss Stevens.

Are you going to give it back to me, Reagan asked, and Miss Stevens did. Reagan held it in her hands, felt the grain of the paper under the ridges of her fingers.

Will you tell me the homework again? she asked.

Miss Stevens stared at her. Reagan remembered what the gin on her teacher's breath had smelled like.

It's easy, Miss Stevens finally said. It's about composition. I want to see a large composition, one with as many figures in it as possible. Different figures. All different kinds of people.

Okay, said Reagan. Thanks.

Think about all the different people you might meet in the world, said Miss Stevens. What they might have to offer you. That's the key to this homework, Reagan.

§

She tried to mentally track Josephine, how much time had passed and how fast she must have been moving on her way to Wherever. The girls' bathroom by the cafeteria, to cry. The low walls around by the dumpsters, just around the corner from the Bad Girls, not so close so as to be associated with them but close enough to get a calming lungful of secondhand smoke. The next class, to endure. They shared a math class; Reagan was on her way across the campus courtyard to the math building. She started to think about what Miss Stevens had said, what thoughts might have made her say it. The bend in the sidewalk came up, and instead of turning right into the math building she kept going straight off of the pavement. She cut across the grass and through the parking lot over the far lawn and over the low fence around the suburban beyond, and if the police liaison caught sight of her at a distance, shadowy ant among the mirror maze of windshield reflectors of senior class cars, he chose to let her go.

Her parents were still at work when she got home; she left them a note saying she was staying at Peter's for the night. Then she snuck upstairs, locked herself in her room, and put the rug into the crack between the carpet and the bottom of the door. She turned off all the lights and dimmed her computer monitor and plugged in headphones to muffle all sound. She had done this before; the first few times she'd been terrified that her parents would check up on her; they never seemed to do so. They didn't this time.

She was reading about Harmon Metzger on Wikipedia, smell of onions and fire salsa from what was probably her dad's dinner working its way up to her, when her headphones beeped; someone had left a message on her Facebook wall. Josephine had sent Reagan a link to the music video of the song Reagan—or the emerald, or whatever—had drawn Josephine listening to.

She sat at her computer and listened to the whole thing twice, three times, and as she listened she wished some affable sociopath programmer would make some technology that would show you if the person of your choice was watching the same YouTube video you were, and if they were, where in the video they were in terms of time, so you could go to that part of the video yourself and watch the same video in perfect secret synchronization, could feel so close to that person, each of you staring at each other from opposite surfaces of the reflecting pond.

She drew a quick picture of Miss Stevens on the paper, leaving plenty of white space. Miss Stevens had anime eyes and a nervous smile and two Sailor Scouts were beaming down at her from either shoulder. After she finished the drawing she looked at it a while, then took off her shirt and looked at herself in the mirror, squinting at herself through the dark, looked at her reflection until her image appeared to lose all meaning, just a series of lines and circles. What had the kid said in class today? A collage of arbitrary flesh. One of her parents was watching some kind of loud action movie, probably sitting on the couch alone, bowl of popcorn being mechanically munched as spies killed terrorists in fictional deserts, explosions casting over affectless face.

She lay down on the bed and set the emerald on her chest, secured the coins on her eyes, felt the breeze through the window tickle her stomach.

§

She dreamed of tigers, their spit running over her like honey, their paws pacing on the sand at the center of tent lined with bleachers and cheering crowds, and in the morning she woke up and saw what she had done.

7

She wants me back, said Reagan, from Peter's floor the next morning as Peter stared at his face in the mirror, inspecting for imperfections. There's no question. That's the only possible interpretation of this Facebook status. The drawing worked perfectly. Before, she thought I was a nuisance. Now she worries I understand her. She can't be indifferent anymore.

This is getting really boring, said Peter. He lay back against his pillow, eyes closed, legs splayed like a rat. So she wants you back. So go back to her. You win; you and your magical emerald win. You lead a perfect life forever.

Reagan sat on the foot of Peter's bed and balanced her Rapidograph against the point where her ankles, Indian-style, came together in a soft cross.

What did you think of her drawing? she asked. Did you think I got her right? Did you think the emerald got her right?

It looked just like her, said Peter.

I mean, did I get her right, said Reagan.

Peter turned on his side and faced the white stucco wall.

God, Peter finally said. I mean it was funny and everything.

What about the new one? asked Reagan. Is that funny?

On the drafting table rested the drawing of Miss Stevens. She crouched, naked, at the center of the drawing, breasts sagging, stretch marks lovingly hatched, her nipples flamboyantly pointed with Muscovite-palace tips. Her partner crouched behind her, naked also. Both were holding bricks and trowels dripping with mortar thick as cake frosting. An army of cartoon characters surrounded them, all naked and all female, whistling as they laid bricks or carried boards and buckets of cement, laughing with eyes psychotically round and bright. They were prepubescent in attitude, jailbait-lush in form; Princess Peach with golden pubic curls accepting a brick from a bosomy Sally Brown, Ayanami and Utena chattering as they ate sack lunches, leaned against the wall, exposed their clear-lined pen-and-ink labial folds; Smurfette's blue thighs wrapped around Gadget's slender white neck as the mouse boosted her up to put the finishing touches on a murder slit in the wall they were building. They were building ramparts, a fortress. Atop them—against an ink-black sky above, her body rendered in the quivery, crosshatched style reserved only for the two adult teachers—rested a whore, an awesome one, lush coiled ringlets cascading from the tiara of skulls at her crown, framing the 666 that burned in her forehead; her striped stockings were torn; her belly was voluptuous with middle age; her rouge was smeared with drybrush; you could smell the olive oil and incense rising from her skin. She was laughing, demon's eyes eerily kind, at the children playing beneath her; she was drinking a martini with three olives speared on a Tarot sword; a fourth olive and a splash of vermouth were about to spill over the rim of her ultra-modern glass into the rising walls. WE ARE BUILDING A BETTER WORLD, bubbled Miss Stevens. Her eyes, lust-wet, were turned on the slender ass of Ariel, bending over gawkily on the new supple legs a witch had given her as she picked up a fresh brick from the pile.

It's, um, said Peter. It's kind of funny.

It's perverted and cruel, said Reagan.

Peter turned on his side again. Reagan kept staring at the pen in her lap.

You were really mad at her, said Peter. It's okay to be mad at someone.

She dedicated her life to teaching ungrateful teenagers, said Reagan. And like, helping troubled queer youth adjust to society. She's a wonderful person.

She watched the folds in Peter's black Burzum T-shirt rise and fall over the bandages across his uppermost ribs.

The emerald did it, she said into space. It's all the emerald. The emerald is destroying everything.

It's hella cursed, said Peter.

It's totally cursed, said Reagan.

You should stop using it, said Peter.

Reagan balanced the Rapidograph against her ankles again and thought about Josephine, one night when they had been watching a movie on Josephine's couch and sat next to each other and after a while she couldn't stand the itch of the space between them anymore, asked if she could put her feet up on Josephine's lap, Josephine agreed; they sat there not speaking and Reagan's naked ankle rested against the soft laundered denim of Josephine's skirt, and here was that ankle now, alone. She thought about it and she thought about her drawing, the vacant music video lyrics echoing off of Josephine's bedroom wall. She felt tired.

§

Despite the pit stop at Peter's en route, she made it to art class early, and with the backpack and its emerald under her feet she sat at her desk and waited for the moment when Josephine would walk in the door. And then here the moment came; Josephine walked in the door, yet the room remained gray. Reagan sat, spine slouched, and watched Josephine cross the room to her desk. For some reason Reagan braced herself, like she expected Josephine to hit her in the face.

I want to talk to you, Josephine said quickly.

Reagan waited for her to say more, but Josephine was waiting for her.

Do you want to meet at Denny's? Reagan asked. The one on the highway? Five o'clock?

Okay, said Josephine. That sounds fine.

Okay, said Reagan. Fine.

How are you doing? Josephine asked. Reagan blinked.

I'm fine, she said. Why?

Josephine shook her head.

No reason, she asked. I was just curious how you were doing.

The class was an anticlimax and Reagan daydreamed through most of it, tried not to look at Miss Stevens and think of the drawing she—or it—had done that morning.

§

The waitress at Denny's rolled her eyes as she set down Reagan's plastic tray of popcorn shrimp, then moved on. Reagan was trying to sketch her from across the restaurant when she saw Josephine walk in the door. She was wearing a light fall jacket and obvious makeup, the kind of thick chalky red lipstick that would grease up your whole lip when she kissed you.

Hi, she said, standing by the booth. Can I sit down?

I invited you here, said Reagan.

Josephine stared at her, smiled tightly, sat down.

Popcorn shrimp, she said. I can't believe you ordered that.

It's Denny's, said Reagan. You have to order gross shit. Do you want something to drink? Have you ever had margaritas? Are they good? You want to order us a round of margaritas? You look older than me even though you're not.

I'll have a Dr. Pepper, Josephine smiled at the waitress. And a salad. No dressing.

They looked at each other. Josephine leaned forward.

So that drawing you did of me, she said.

What about it, asked Reagan.

It was me, wasn't it? asked Josephine. It was really, really something. It was really beautiful.

Reagan blinked and let the breading fall off a piece of shrimp; this was unexpected.

The drawing was incredibly mean, said Reagan. I'm sorry. I was angry at you.

Don't apologize, said Josephine. It wasn't mean. You were totally right about me.

Reagan dug her thumbnail into the edge of the paper placemat, made crosshatch designs in the lush pictures of bacon and fried cheese sticks penetrating dips.

Like, that's what someone of substance is like in today's culture, Josephine said. Kind of in the world, but not of the world. Where you made me look sort of bored, but sort of sad.

Reagan dug her nail harder into the placemat.

I'm not using my potential, Josephine continued. It's like I have to rise above the boredom of suburbia to really succeed. Like all those people in the classroom who didn't get what you'd done and why it was so beautiful. All the books you included—that was amazing, how you knew just what books to put there. How you just—knew me.

It's fine, said Reagan, looking at her shrimp. Jesus. You don't have to rise above anything.

How did you know that about me? asked Josephine.

I don't know, muttered Reagan. I guessed. I'm sorry.

They sat and loud guitars thumped out of the restaurant PA.

I missed you, said Josephine.

Her eyes were on Reagan's hand, the one not picking at her placemat, the one that was grinding the cap of her vestigial Rapidograph into the tabletop.

Reagan let herself give into this. She let the conversation drift—into memories of good times, into confessions of isolation, into analysis of the past and its imagined crimes and imagined prophetic moments of future happiness, perfect understanding—and she let herself make jokes, let herself creep up on flirtation, let herself ask for the popcorn shrimp to go, let the two of them split the check down the middle all even-steven, let herself walk close to the swinging arm of Josephine's fall jacket, let herself set the Styrofoam box of popcorn shrimp on the ground to hug Josephine goodbye, let herself know what it meant when Josephine closed her eyes and leaned slightly, very slightly in, let herself take the opening and let herself respond, let herself lose control a little at the warm slide of mouths, the hidden resistance of the blood vessel or nerve or whatever it was pulsing just beneath the skin of Josephine's lower lip, let herself breathe hoarsely and hang in the moment, then another. And she imagined the word bubble oozing out of Josephine's mouth and into hers: I AM A YOUNG WOMAN OF SUBSTANCE. She was suddenly very aware of Josephine's spit in her mouth; she broke away.

What? asked Josephine, alarmed. She put a hand on Reagan's shoulder and Reagan flinched away.

The date was over; on the ground, red ants roved and swarmed over the popcorn exterior of the shrimp.

8

She was taking off her shoes in the front hall when her father came down the stairs.

Did you forget anything today, he asked her.

She walked past him into the kitchen. The counters were clean, scrubbed stark; she took out the milk and poured a tall glass. He followed her in, white socks on clean tiles.

Are you ignoring me? he asked. Is that what we're going to do?

I don't think I forgot anything, Reagan said. I'm sorry. I did really well in art class the other day. My picture was up at the front of the room. It was so good the teacher thought I totally plagiarized it. I won, the other day.

You did forget something, her father said. What did you forget.

She leaned on the counter and let the milk touch her lips, after a moment drank some of it.

Do you need me to tell you? he asked.

She set the milk down.

Garbage, he said. You forgot your garbage.

It's not Monday, she said. —And I already did last week.

I asked you to do it Friday, said her father. I asked you on Monday. Because we're entertaining Friday. Your mother doesn't think we entertain enough so we're going to fucking entertain Friday. And that's fine, you said. No problem, daaad, you said. Yes sir right away sir. We had an oral contract, Reagan.

She closed her eyes; she always wondered what it was about her voice that made him want to imitate it. His imitation didn't even sound like her. It was the same insulting generic imitation he used for everyone.

Do you really not remember this? her father asked. Are you having memory problems generally? Are you on drugs, maybe, and they're affecting your memory?

I'm not on drugs, she said.

He looked at her. He didn't look like her; she'd always wondered about this.

It's a pretty shitty way to treat someone, he said. Meaning no offense. Stating the facts. It's pretty shitty not to give someone the credit of remembering what they ask you to do.

I'm sorry, she said. I seriously didn't remember. I'm really sorry, dad. Okay?

I'm sorry, daaad, he imitated. Then: What am I supposed to do about that?

She forced herself to drink the rest of the milk, fast as she could, her throat dry. Then she took her glass to the sink, poured it out, washed it, let it drip and breathed, a moment later dried it, carefully, with paper towels, put it away, upside down, as was right.

I'm sorry, she said again. I'll take out the garbage right now.

Go ahead, he said.

She looked under the kitchen sink. There was a fresh and empty bag in the trash can. Her father looked back at her, his eyes beestung.

There's nothing here, she said.

Nope, he said.

Where is the trash, she asked.

I don't remember, he said.

She waited; he kept looking at her. He had a weird little smile.

I'm going up to my room, she said.

Okay, he said. That's a good idea.

She went to her room, where she hadn't slept for two days. Two long black bags of trash, kitchen and bathroom, lay on their sides on her carpet. He hadn't tied them before tossing them here, and some napkins, food debris, different things had spilled onto the carpet. He came up the stairs behind her, then tossed two fresh folded black trash bags onto the floor beside her with a plastic slap, then went back downstairs without a word.

There weren't any flies that she could see. She looked at the bags a long time, like a mother deer she'd struck with her car, ruins of her windshield sparkling against its side and drying blood matting its perfect tawny fur in ways that could never be made better. She thought about leaving the bags there, sleeping at the center of the weird spoiling penumbra, becoming sick with strange garbage disease, body purpling and cracking open in shattered cysts; at what point would her father feel sorry for her? She couldn't think of a point at which he would feel sorry for her. This was a childish way to be thinking, and it'd be worse if he decided to clean it up himself; she was surprised he hadn't already come back into her room and started doing that. She got to work, repacking the fallen trash into the fresh bags, lifting old rumpled sponges and paper towel rolls, scooping food waste from the wet loops of carpet; she made the exterior of the bag into a kind of glove and felt the weight of spoilage in her hand, gagged on the last drops of milk in her throat. She left the light in the hallway on when she humped the bags down the stairs and out to the city cans by the garage; when she got back the hallway light was out. He'd come to check on her work. She'd done a lot of it wrong, stains and chunks and particles she hadn't fully eliminated. She went downstairs and got paper towels and scouring products and she worked for fifteen, twenty minutes and thought there was no way he could find a problem with her now. The initial problem was over; no way it could ever be made better, but there was no other way he could find to hurt her, she figured.

She tried to remember why she'd been in such a good mood when she got home, remembered the iPod songs from Josephine's dashboard speakers.

She sat at the drafting table, nostrils so scoured out by products that they burned at the back, and in quick sketchy snaps of the Rapidograph she drew cartoons of herself and Josephine kissing in the parking lot. She bit her lip and worked on the technical problems—whose cheek overlapped whose, how to resolve the tangle of lines where hair met hair, how matching sets of noses and breasts ought to look in perspective and relative to one another. As she drew her shoulders started to get limber again and her room got dark so gradually she didn't even notice when she had to switch on the lamp, like the white paper itself was glowing behind her lines.

She looked down at the drawing, remembered, smiled. She looked at it for a long time. The longer she looked, the fainter her smile got, until finally it went out, a dot of candle fire drowning in undrained wax, and the dimple lines shrank into nothing and reappeared on her forehead instead.

The emerald was still in the pouch of her backpack, resting on her bed.

She went to her computer, dismissed the screen saver, checked her Facebook. Josephine had posted a song to her wall again. Some lady was singing brightly over a harp with what she guessed were pop touches. Reagan's bedroom smelled like lemons and this song sounded too sweet for any real human feeling. She tried to make it through but turned it off halfway without thinking about it.

It occurred to her that she had achieved everything she had ever wanted.

§

She let herself be kicked around by waves of Internet surf for an hour, hour and a half, until she was only reading every fifth line of different blogs. The drawing was still on the table; the bag with the emerald in it was still on the bed. She picked it up, put it in the closet, pulled back the covers, lay on the bed.

She tried to make herself fall asleep and couldn't. There was a little stack of paperbacks by her bed; she picked one up and read five, six pages of it before realizing she didn't care about what she was reading; she had managed to remember none of it. She did the same with another book, then another; same results. She lay on her side and tried by force to think logically incoherent things, dream things.

§

At some point she must have succeeded because the numbers on her alarm clock jumped ahead. Her parents' TV had gone silent; her mouth tasted sour, bad. The room still smelled like lemons and garbage. She got up and went to the drafting table. The drawing of herself kissing Josephine lay spread out and defenseless in the light of the lamp she hadn't turned off.

I am sleepwalking, she made herself think, even convinced herself of it.

She went to the closet, skin cold with sweat. She took out the emerald and watched the light of the drafting table shine within its dark angles. It was hot in her hand.

§

In the morning she shut off her alarm on the first ring and took the emerald from her chest, rubbed the sore place on her sternum where it had rested. She set it on the pillow beside her, strange mineral bedmate, and she closed her eyes and decided not to wake up. Waking up would mean living in a world in which whatever had happened before you went to bed could not be changed.

On the page: Reagan, voluptuously sprawled naked on a Louis XIV throne, stains on the upholstery between her legs. Josephine, impeccable, sucking her toes. A second Josephine braided Reagan's hair. A third licked her vagina. I'M GAY FOR REAGAN, one said. I LOVE YOU UNCONDITIONALLY, said the second. MMRPH MMF MM MMRH, said the third. Cartoon Reagan's mouth lolled open in total satisfaction, her eyes rolled back, half in ecstasy, half directed toward God in a kind of celestial mad dogging, curls dangling around her ears like the mane of a lion. It was beautiful; it was like a stained glass window of a saint at the moment of greatest martyrial ecstasy, holy light shooting out of her eyes, ears, head. In a doorway drawn behind the scene, a second Reagan stood, drooling and slavering at the sight of herself being worshipped, supporting herself on the frame of the door, bags of garbage heaped around herself like a soldier's sandbag wall.

She tore the drawing in two, but someone could still put it back together, couldn't they, so she tore it again, again, again, again, crumpled half the pieces and threw them out the window; there would be dew on the grass; they would dissolve, become part of the soil, grow evil trees that would provide evil shade. The rest she burned with a lighter and let them disassemble in the holder of an old candle, fire white and toxic from the chemicals that kept the surface of the paper, smoke black.

She went into the bathroom. Her face in the mirror still looked like her face in the cartoon. She put her face close to the mirror so it no longer looked like a face, closed her eyes and brought it back, opened her eyes and drew a lipstick cartoon over her outlines.

9

That whole weekend she worked on the composition assignment. Her phone buzzed and chirped and she ignored it; she endured the required lunches and dinners her father asked for—he asked her over and over how her room smelled lately; she sat there quietly eating and she got back to the table as quickly as she could.

She figured out early on that all the emerald required to activate was her sleeping long enough to dream; time didn't matter; black circles sprouted from her eyes as she napped and dreamed late—two, three, four in the morning, sunrise, in oils, acrylics, pastels, gouaches, straight up Crayola, old Portishead and PJ Harvey CDs marking the time with track repeats—and she never slept so well under the emerald's influence, so when she woke up to the alarm—or didn't wake up, tossed and hit the snooze button and lost hours—she sometimes found it hard to know if the crosshatched black-and-white stuff invariably on her drafting table in the morning was some kind of REM holdover, some monochrome dog's dream. But it was all real. It refused to go away no matter how hard she stared at it.

§

The assignment was due Tuesday; she missed art class Monday. She wandered onto campus around lunch and yawned through the cafeteria line, then took a table by herself and tried to get the lines of her classmates' faces right as she sketched them in Rapidograph from across the cafeteria.

Hi, said Josephine. Is this taken?

She sat down without Reagan saying anything, cool red sunglasses crimping her nose. Reagan had never known Josephine to eat in the cafeteria. Now Josephine was here, on the other side of the picture windows from the duck pond with her, shifting her sunglasses to her untanned forehead.

Hey, said Josephine. What're you drawing?

Reagan finished as many lines as she thought she could get away with before putting her pen down.

Kids, she said. Other kids. It's for that assignment.

Josephine bit her lip and looked at the table, then looked back up.

For the composition assignment? she asked. For Miss Stevens?

Yeah, said Reagan. I'm going to draw everyone I know in one big drawing and see what comes out.

Comes out? asked Josephine.

In terms of composition, said Reagan quickly.

Josephine nodded and frowned at the drawing a little, like she was evaluating it. Reagan picked up her pen and put it to the end of one of the lines.

I came in here to find you, said Josephine. Do you maybe want to go sit by the duck pond? And talk?

Talk about what, said Reagan, rolling the pen between her fingers.

Us, shrugged Josephine. The weather. Whatever we want to talk about.

Reagan looked at her. And suddenly she saw the Josephine of her drawing—mouth wet, slightly open, fire licking her irises as her tongue licked Reagan, heavy, lazy eyelids. The cartoon lines hung in space, superimposed over the mostly smooth Clearasil skin, the tiny rim of down on her nostrils, the blank and bright and waiting expression. Her mind turned without prompting to stretch and twist and bend the lines of the drawing to fit the real contours of the face, double exposure.

I really want to work on this assignment, she said.

Fine, said Josephine, eyes blinking. Fine. That's fine. Some other time.

She didn't get up, neither did she take out a book or a phone or anything to do. Neither did Reagan pick up the pen; she kept rolling it in her fingers. She looked at the knot of the scarf around Josephine's neck, halfway between the drawing of the student and Josephine's living face, looking at Reagan's. Finally she started drawing again until eventually Josephine went away.

10

She skipped dinner and blew off an invitation from Peter. She read about Harmon Metzger instead, an old *Comics Journal* interview she dug up online. Strictly speaking it wasn't about Metzger so much as about a lot of different underground comix figures of the past, Crumb and Shelton and Wilson and Moscoso, and tucked into the back, Metzger. The Metzger part had been completed something like two years before he went, and it read like a preemptive obituary; there were lots of details about his shaking hands, the grime on his table, the way he sponged money for a pastry from the interviewer. Weirdly, he spent the interview talking almost not at all about PHUCKBOOK PHUNNIES, the one book anyone really remembered. Instead he talked about a very early story he had done, when he was nineteen or something, a story that had ended up published dozens of years after the fact due to a quirky legal situation with one of Metzger's siblings who'd claimed rights to it somehow in the wake of a dodgy land deal both had been involved in.

This early piece was the story of a sad rejected boy who decides one day to dig a hole deeper than anyone has ever dug before. Mebbe there's a better world at the bottom! read the lettering, impeccable even at nineteen. When this rejected boy strikes the earth with his shovel he hits a water main; floods and raw damage pour out and the foam and pressure sweep him away. Clinging to an old tire to keep his head up, contra physics, he follows the water downhill and downstream, into the sewers, through an open culvert into sudden daylight, a strange creek, a stream, rivers. The vegetation becomes bizarre, twisted Joshua trees mixed with jungles and cannibal flowers in living Prismacolor, the glass towers of New York disappearing in bright silhouette. Ho, hum!, he says. Guess there ain't nothing for it but to keep drifting!

He falls asleep, there on the river. And he dreams. And he wakes up when his tire jars to a stop. The river has narrowed, boiled away; he is in the desert; he can not get back the way he came; the sun is burning down. Where once the river carried him, now he must walk or he will die.

He finds a cave and goes into the shadows, out of the sun. Comically, there's a line of washing hung in front of this cave to dry in the sand: scraps of dress, women's things. Funny!, he says. I haven't ever yet seen a brassiere without a woman t' hold it up! A page is spent detailing his musings on the bra, different angles on it, before he slips into the cave hoping to steal some food. But as he walks—illuminating the way ahead with a lighter he's somehow kept dry in his pocket for the whole length of the river—he sees the walls are painted. At first all he notices is that the paintings are done in some kind of berry juice; there are a couple of slapsticky pages of him kind of bestially devouring this work, on his knees licking it off the rock. He sits, sated, against a rock along the cave passageway, licking his lips. There are still paintings left he hasn't eaten. He looks at them and he realizes they're beautiful. There are pages of complicated, comically-depicted guilt and self-loathing, the boy's figure contorting on the floor of the cave. All I can do is destroy, he cringes. I've never made a beautiful thing in my life—buuuurp—

A loud yawn wakes him up, draws him further down the tunnel. And here it is, a full page: The artist who paints in berry juice lies there asleep on the hide of a lion; her hair long and black and curtained over the rock floor, curves bubbling out of her long frame like grace notes. Her face when sleeping is permanently dimpled; a pale cat dreams curled in the corner next to a bowl made of a dried and hollowed out cactus, cured iguana steaks and desert roots gathered in its base, jars of berry paint on all the shelves. This young bestial man stands in the doorway of the cave watching her, Prismacolor purple on his lips, staring at her and the jars of paint. The magazine had a reproduction of this panel, no border around it, no black, no white at all, just fields of colored pencil strokes bleeding out into infinity.

The comic goes kind of downhill from there. The boy trips or sneezes or something and wakes the girl up; they have a conversation that makes it plain that Harmon Metzger had pretty much never talked to an actual woman ever; the action gets pornographic in a way that isn't explicit but that's somehow much worse for that; there's a convoluted part where they have to construct a power boat to fight the current back up the river to the city. In the final panel they are married and presumably will be happy forever. My troubles! Heck! Who needs them?, the boy says, winking out of the fourth wall at the reader in a way that suggests some kind of minor demon or Mafia flunky.

Metzger said in the interview that the book had allowed him to lose his virginity, and that shortly afterward he had stopped drawing in color.

The interviewer said that was a shame, that this had been a fantastic and beautiful piece of work.

Metzger said he hated it.

The interviewer said he couldn't understand why.

Metzger said, I used to believe in a lot of awful things about the world.

§

The interview said nothing about the emerald. How had it come to him? Had he been given it by some eccentric mentor, let its curse curdle his work for secret years? Had he bought it, intended to give it as a fucked up dowry to some dream lover, some sleepy eyed cave woman of his own? Had he found the thing? Had he made the thing? Had it formed out of melancholy and bile in his stomach like a gallstone vomited into existence one black day? Where did something like the emerald come from?

I I

Reagan's work wasn't hanging at the front of the room when she walked in for the Tuesday critique. A long roll of butcher paper hung there instead, extending all the way across the whiteboard. The upper and lower thirds of the paper had been left white; the middle was a band of glossy photos of celebrities, probably X-actoed out of different magazines, arranged from fattest in the west of the room to most skeletal in the east with infinite subtle gradations of body image in between.

Reagan suffered silently through the classroom discussion of this work. One of the pop star celebs in the composition had just died in the process of moving from west to east along the butcher paper, and there was a debate about whether the very voyage was responsible for her death, also what her best song had been. Reagan tried to imagine her drawing hanging at the front of the room, what might be said about it. She felt like she was thinking through a fog; she felt like sleeping.

At the end of the hour Miss Stevens handed out the slips of paper with grades on them. See me, hers said, in red marker.

A note landed on her desk, folded into a delicate jet plane. She opened it up. I miss you, it said. She looked over at Josephine, who was staring back at her, chewing a pencil. Josephine raised her hand slowly. Reagan shot a weary thumbs up and looked away.

§

The school counselor was there in Miss Stevens's office, a stocky woman with tall blond hair and sharp executive eyes over a heavily stretched T-shirt featuring Christmas cats. Her eyes did not change as she arranged her mouth warmly. She was sitting in Miss Stevens's desk with a truly massive mug of cold coffee in front of her, a photograph of Bob Geldof cheaply printed on it with a word balloon saying *Tell Me Why I Don't Like Mondays!* Miss Stevens was standing by the ficus, one shoe turned in toward the other and pretending to read her calendar. Reagan's drawing was spread over a desk in the corner, its corners weighted carefully with books and cups of pencils so as to obscure as little of the drawing as possible.

Hi, Reagan, said the counselor. I'm Mrs. Fawkes. I don't believe we've ever spoken before. I think it's important that we change that now.

I guess so, said Reagan.

Why don't you sit down, smiled Mrs. Fawkes. Would you like some water? A napkin? Are you comfortable? Need anything?

Are we going to talk about my drawing? Reagan asked.

Oh, yes, said Mrs. Fawkes. We are going to talk very seriously about this drawing. If that's all right with you.

The drawing had emerged through a kind of dialectic process between her and the emerald; the first pass had been honestly sloppy and Reagan had corrected it with light ink wash, white gouache, little arrows and stick figures as kind of editorial notes for the emerald, delivered in a series of draining catnaps during which she and the curse hammered out the work between them. The product of their labors was a seventeen by seventeen square of Bristol board that presented a kind of Hieronymous Bosch amusement park, one attended not only by everyone in her art class, but also by the generally accepted core of the honors program school-wide, all of Josephine's friends. Most of them were engaged in some kind of Dantean pursuit. A plump boy fumbled with a hammer aimed at the bell of a strength tester, an octet of slender braceface girls danced around him with arms linked like a maypole as the crotch of his Dockers burst into frustrated fire, four blond jocks with eyes closed in ecstasy and spiked collars around their throats circled a tall ice cream sundae on all fours, at the center of the vanilla scoop the student council president, a smart cheerleader, a cherry around her neck. Anarcho-vegan kids dangled like acrobats from power lines and the bulk of the student body coursed through the colored carnival sky on a dangerous looking all-wood roller coaster, cell phones at their ears and Louis Wain lightning showing which kids were talking to which. Harvard-bound Mike sat on a throne of skulls in a cloud above the proceedings, wearing a ringmaster's hat and tossing handfuls of coins to the unlucky ones below. The forced perspective she'd chosen let her show both the girls throwing up in the coaster's crossbeams and the obvious queer kid cutting his distorted throat in the hall of mirrors with an equally distorted razor; the eye—guided around the black-and-white maze with the affability of a museum docent in rough order of comparative immorality of subject, then turned loose in the lobby gift shop—couldn't decide which depiction to rest on. All the kids had been drawn with vacant cartoon o's for eyes, their jaws and necks overstimulated, taut. All the kids had diplomas stuffed in their pockets. On the far side of the fence you could just make out Josephine, suspended, her hands dangling between loops of razor wire like a puppy yearning to get in. The edges of the paper were black, scorched with fire.

Sure, said Reagan. Let's talk about my drawing.

Miss Stevens turned a page of her calendar forward and then turned it back, not looking at Reagan.

Why don't you tell me, using your own words, what this is a drawing of, she said.

It was an assignment, said Reagan. I worked really hard.

You were assigned to draw this subject? asked Mrs. Fawkes. Or a subject of your choice? Why did you draw your fellow students this way?

What way? asked Reagan. Crosshatched?

Mrs. Fawkes smiled, exhaled, looked at her coffee.

Hurting themselves and each other, she finally said.

Reagan frowned at Miss Stevens's back.

It was a composition assignment, she said finally. This is just—

their composition.

Reagan, said Miss Stevens; she may have been looking at Reagan now, though Reagan was no longer looking at her. This is really serious, okay? There are things we can't ignore in this drawing.

Such as the boy with the knife at his throat, Mrs. Fawkes said, and swigged her coffee from her Bob Geldof mug.

It's just a drawing, said Reagan. This is stupid. I have class.

No, you don't have class, actually, said Mrs. Fawkes.

Reagan stared at Mrs. Fawkes's legs—sheer sausage-skin nylon, the mesh straining over her cellulite legs—and she stared at her own legs, too long now by three or four years probably to dangle from the orange plastic seat over the linoleum.

Look, said Mrs. Fawkes. You're a smart girl. So I'll ask you straight out. There's a drawing of a boy cutting up his neck in a mirror. Tell me about this boy. Do you have strong feelings about this person? Is he maybe a boy you have strong feelings for? Maybe you like this boy?

One of Reagan's hands was shaking; she grabbed it with the other and held it in place.

I don't belong here, she said. I should be in class.

Mrs. Fawkes tapped her foot, rolled her eyes, drank from her mug.

Your parents will be here soon, Reagan, said Miss Stevens, after remaining silent for a while.

§

She wanted her mother to show up first, but after ten minutes mostly spent looking at the floor while Miss Stevens stared at nothing and Mrs. Fawkes traced over the drawing with her finger—outlining carnage with the nail, humming Christmas songs to herself—the doorknob turned and from the way Reagan's neck tensed she knew it was her father, and that it would only be her father. He didn't look at her beyond a quick peripheral glimpse. He smiled a broad and friendly smile at Mrs. Fawkes;

she smiled back and took his hand. There were introductions. So what is it Reagan's done, he asked.

She knew better than to talk as Mrs. Fawkes gave her father a guided tour of the drawing. He didn't say much as she pointed out the specific students she could recognize, the details. He sighed wearily at certain extreme points—like the cheerleader sundae, Reagan guessed, and the class president chasing his girlfriend with a vacuum cleaner brandished over his head, eyes hypno-spirals—hummed, clucked his teeth, like someone describing a bad trip to the DMV or a home decoration disaster.

You can see, then, that we have a problem, said Mrs. Fawkes. One the school has to take seriously.

She wasn't looking at her father but knew he was smiling his apology-to-strangers smile. She tried not to think bad thoughts about him. She was the one in trouble now.

I'm truly sorry, he said. I think you've taken all the right measures and I sure appreciate you bringing this to my attention. She can be a real handful and I'm just really and truly sorry you've had to deal with her.

Mrs. Fawkes adjusted her lips, restored her smile. Miss Stevens didn't move.

Of course, Mrs. Fawkes said. So yes. So I can assume that you'll pursue some kind of—assessment, or counseling, to address the problem, on your own. Outside of school. In addition to what counseling the school can provide.

You don't need to provide any counseling, her father said. You've had to deal with so much already. I'll take it from here. I can assure you, you won't see another drawing like that again.

Mrs. Fawkes cleared her throat and stared at Reagan's father. He turned up his smile. Reagan watched him do it.

The school hardly minds, Mrs. Fawkes said, shortly. I'd be happy to talk to Reagan directly about this any time she wants. Reagan, I would be happy to talk to you directly.

Reagan tried to meet the counselor's eyes, but her father was in the way, a business casual eclipse. She stared at her feet.

Reagan, are you comfortable with what's happening? asked

Miss Stevens.

Sure, said Reagan. It'd be worse if she said anything else.

Okay, said Mrs. Fawkes, and picked up her mug, set it against her lip, peeked out over its rim. Okay. Then we'll leave it with a two week suspension. I'll give you some referrals. And we'll see where we go from there.

Sounds fantastic, beamed her father, and then he turned his face to Reagan. She wished he wouldn't; his eyes were on her, but looking inward; his teeth were white, their even orthodontia split down the middle of his lower jaw.

What do you say, kiddo? he asked her. Want to get out of here?

She looked at Miss Stevens; the art teacher was watching her. —Sure, kiddo, Reagan said.

Reagan, said Miss Stevens. I need to talk to you a moment first about the homework for the time off. Could you come into the classroom?

Reagan got up. Her father waited for her with Mrs. Fawkes as she went into the classroom with Miss Stevens.

Bob Geldof, her father said as the door was closing. Oldie but goodie.

She could hear the guidance counselor laughing politely through the crack in space.

§

Miss Stevens gestured Reagan over to the side, away from the window. In the empty classroom she grabbed her around the shoulders, threw her sneakers off balance. Reagan bent her elbows at her sides, bent them to bring her wrists up, stiffly, along either side of Miss Stevens's torso. She hugged her teacher like she was feeling her way around a marble column, like if she wasn't extra careful the pieces of some statue would topple onto her head. She thought of the drawing of the art teacher among the young cartoon girls and she flinched, but her teacher held on.

It's going to be okay, said Miss Stevens.

The door to the office opened and her father stepped out. She waited for Miss Stevens to let go; Miss Stevens didn't let go. It was left to Reagan to let go. She stiffened her legs and pushed away.

Miss Stevens relaxed her grip. Her eyes were wet, anime eyes. Reagan gave a short nod, acknowledging the hug. Miss Stevens nodded back.

It's going to be fine, Reagan said to her teacher.

I 2

They were sitting in the family car. Other times she had been stuck in the family car with her father and she had at least been able to check the speed of the car, to multiply it by roughly how far away their destination was, add in the Global Traffic Factor from the table of constants that she'd thought up on a car trip when she was twelve and that she kept loosely in her head, and from all of this calculate how much time she'd be trapped with him. Right now he had unfolded her drawing over the steering wheel and was looking at it again. The engine was off. The air between the windows, broiled in parking lot sun, was starting to choke her.

Looks slick, he finally said. He folded the drawing into sharp quarters and set it on the back seat; she wanted to take it but knew better than to reach or to ask. —Looks like a heavy metal album cover or something.

Those are exciting, she allowed.

He nodded to himself and looked out the windshield, glare reflecting from the mirrored sun screen of the car in front of him into his glasses.

Which psychiatrist are you going to make me see, she asked.

The key was in the ignition already. Air conditioning hissed in as soon as he started the car; he put it into drive, then sat there, foot on the brake, wrists resting on the wheel.

I'm not making you see a shrink, he said, tired. What point

would there be in that?

Reagan stared at the dashboard. —They seemed to think something was wrong, she said.

Don't be naïve, said her father. These school administrators smell politics in the wind. Always thinking about the next Columbine or Sandy Hook or something. Ever hear of CYA procedures? Cover-your-ass. There's nothing wrong with my kid's head. You just did a fucked up drawing and turned it in as an assignment. Not smart, but not crazy.

What about the doctor's note, asked Reagan.

You let me worry about that, said her father.

They sat, the air conditioning separating the strands of her eyebrows.

I'm glad you understand that nothing's wrong with me, said Reagan hollowly.

I understand that you got yourself suspended for doing something not smart, said her father. I understand you've basically shot yourself in the foot when it comes to colleges. These things I understand.

She stared into the vent, tried to trace back the vectors of air striking her to their source somewhere in the dark inner parts of the car.

I mean it's not like your chances were so hot anyway, my child, he said. You don't have many AP classes. You're slumming it in the ones you do have. You should basically be planning on a couple years community college straight out of high school so a four year college has a prayer of one day taking you, if you're lucky, if you think you can get your grades up. But now this. But now—he sighed—now, I don't know if even community college is a possibility for us anymore.

Lots of people get into community college, Reagan said.

You're not lots of people, said her father.

She stared into the vent and tried not to move. Finally, mercifully, he decided to take his foot off the brake and shift the car back into reverse. They were moving.

You smell terrible, he said after a moment. Did you stop washing your hair? Did we really raise you so as to believe that that wasn't a requirement?

She didn't say anything.

Why did you do this? he asked. Are your mother and I that bad as parents? Is that why you're punishing us? You used to be a very good daughter, all things considered. You used to not do things like this, punish us like this. You used to be very quiet and respectful.

You and mom aren't bad parents, Reagan said in a monotone.

We must be pretty shitty parents, said her father. Why else would you be treating us so shittily? Not to mention yourself. Why else would you be taking steps like this, deliberately fucking up your life and chances?

I'm not taking steps, Reagan said.

Taking steps, continued her father, —like, I don't know, count 'em, deliberately fucking up your grades, fucking up your room, making fucking drawings that get the school fucking shrink all up in my case—

Jesus, shouted Reagan, —none of this is even about you—and her head lurched to the side, whacked against the passenger door, as her father, his face twisted up and his eyes crazy with the tyranny of a child, twisted the wheel, swerved off the road and onto a side street, pushed the brakes to the floor and skidded to a stop in front of a strange and quiet suburban house.

I'll start driving again, her father said after a while, —when you're ready to talk like an adult, rather than to whine and scream like a baby.

Reagan flung herself back upright in her seat, adjusted her seat belt, rubbed the side of her skull, pressed her teeth into one another.

Baby hurt her head, her father said. His brows were wrinkled. Baby had a really bad day and made a mean old drawing and shit her crib.

She sat still; she wished she hadn't been stupid and gotten herself into this situation.

Keep it up, he said quietly. We'll sit here forever. We'll never get home.

And it was true; he would do it; he would wait here as long as she and her bad nature let him. He was stronger than her, larger than her; she would die first when they ran out of food and water; he would be here long after she was gone. She was weaker than him. She was weak and she let him do this to her. There was nothing she could do but do the Right Thing, which was shut up, sit as still as she could, leave three fingers pressed to the throb on the side of her skull, try to wait until her feeling got cold enough for her to be the adult in the situation. His breath seethed on like a metronome, unchanged, and she could feel herself becoming okay with it. She could feel herself becoming sad for him. She could feel the throb in her head. She should stop being cruel to him all the time, she thought, like a ray of sun breaking through a cloud on the cover of an evangelical tract. The thought made her feel full of white light.

I'm sorry I acted like a child, she told her father.

He nodded and released the brake. Gently he guided the car back into traffic. Neither of them spoke. If nothing else crazy happened it would take forty miles per hour divided by sixty for minutes and times one point five miles times Global Traffic Factor of 2 for rush hour to get home.

Your art teacher, said her father. Is she a lesbian?

I don't know, said Reagan, feeling her skull.

She seems like she could be, said her father. I'm not being offensive by saying that. She has short hair. She hugged you. She chose a career that put her around lots of attractive teenage girls. These are facts about her. You need to be careful about her.

Yes, said Reagan.

They pulled into the garage. She got out. He put his hand on her shoulder.

Wait, he said.

She looked at him. He picked up the folded drawing and handed it to her.

Is your head okay? he asked.

It's fine, she said.

I 3

Finally he let her go out of the car. She went into the house with him still in the garage and thought: This is the one moment I can scream, before he comes in the door. She went upstairs to her room. It was clean and empty. She closed the door behind her and put her back on the door and thought: They care about me. She slid her back down the door until she was sitting on the carpet and her eyes found it hard to focus.

When your eyes can't focus you see strange things in a stucco wall. The spectral faces of cowboys. Witches. Ivy and coral snaking in subterranean forests. All of it glowing, never black, skating like many-colored oil pools over a pure white wall.

§

Her father had gone into his office; complicated Iron Maiden songs poured from his speakers. He liked *Run For The Hills* because it was about how the Indians had suffered. After a while, she went to the computer and searched for therapists in her town. She tried to imagine her father doing the same thing, which one he would pick for her. If he would pick any of them for her.

After some time, she went into her bookmarks and read the long piece on Harmon Metzger again. She was reading it when her mother came in. Her mother's hair was down, tumbling like brush ends from the hood of a sweatshirt from some long-ago-visited touristy mountain.

Hi, her mother said. What're you doing?

Reading, she said.

I see, said her mother. Reading about what?

Famous comic book artists, said Reagan. American heroes.

I see, said her mother.

Reagan smiled and turned back to the computer. She read the same paragraph three times, then turned around. Her mother was still there.

What is it? she asked. Did you have a good day at work?

Yeah, said her mother. Definitely. Thanks for asking.

No problem, said Reagan.

The computer buzzed; Iron Maiden wailed.

Can we talk about what happened at school today? her mother asked. There was some trouble?

I made a drawing the school counselor didn't like, said Reagan. So they want me to stay here for a couple of weeks, then go back. And everything'll be fine. Just like it always was, mom.

Why didn't the teacher like your drawing? her mother asked.

I don't know, said Reagan.

That's too bad, said her mother. People should always like what you do.

Reagan looked at her mother. Her mother looked at the screen, at her own bangs.

Did you talk to your father already, she said nervously.

We talked, Reagan said.

Did you say you were sorry, her mother asked.

Sure, said Reagan. Then, heedlessly: —He hit me in the skull, really hard. Or, or his car door did. It hurt a whole lot.

He ran you over with the car? her mother asked, alarmed.

No, said Reagan. It was just kind of a bump while I was in the car. I guess he didn't mean to do it.

Oh, her mother said. That's a relief. I'm glad you already talked to him.

Reagan watched her; she didn't look relieved. She looked as if she would have been happy if Reagan's dad really had run her over with the car. Like that would have been an action you couldn't ignore anymore; like that would have been a doorway.

Do you want to see my drawing? Reagan suddenly asked.

She took the folded Bristol board and stretched it out to its full length. Her mother stared at it, face falling.

I wonder what people would say, if they knew you drew them this way, her mother said finally.

Reagan didn't say anything; she watched her mother instead of the lines on the paper.

Well, her mother smiled, without using her eyes. I'll see you at dinner. Keep your head down.

She stopped in the doorway.

You've got a better life than you realize you do, she said, and Reagan turned to look at her mother. She smiled. Her teeth were straight, her clothes were new and clean. She had been to college. She worked a good and rewarding job. There was dinner waiting on the table for her.

When she went out she left the door open behind her. Reagan stared into the hallway until her mother went down the stairs, and then she went forward and closed the door as quietly as she could.

§

She sat on the floor as Iron Maiden played and ran out, as the TV switched on and the newscaster blared. Then she got up and taped her drawing to the wall, half on the door and half on the stucco, like sealing the door of a pyramid.

She picked up the phone and dialed the area code, then the first six digits of Josephine's number. She took her finger away from the keypad, let the phone rest like a coin in her hand. She bounced it up and down in her palm, twice. She closed her eyes and moved her finger in a circle. Eyes closed, she brought her finger down on the keypad once more, then brought the phone to her ear, then opened her eyes.

It rang three times before someone picked up.

Brookes Landscaping, said a harried male voice on the line, young by the crack in his voice, young like her.

She closed her eyes again and let the phone hang in her palm until the kid got tired of saying Brookes Landscaping at her and hung up.

Below her, dinner conversation was happening. She got up and went to the drafting table, took out paper, began working on a drawing of her father.

§

No one called her to dinner. The food her mother cooked for her sat on the table, slowly went cold, was scraped into the garbage, was put under the sink waiting to be thrown away and forgotten.

She wrote a letter to Peter; she posted on Josephine's wall, just a heart. She wrote a number on a piece of paper, the number of days before she would graduate high school and the world was before her. She crossed the number out and drew a zero, went over it with her pen once, twice, three times, until the paper tore.

The drawing of her father sat on the corner like a seed tucked just under the surface of fresh soil, incubating under the heat of the swivel lamp.

She slept cradling the emerald in her arms.

14

In her dream, Reagan was inside the black emerald. She wore a Victorian dress with a bustle and carried a parasol, and a veil fluttered over her face. The emerald spun like a UFO, but inside it its revolution felt slow, stately, as if Reagan was having an elegant meal in a revolving restaurant. It had grown a comfortable crystal chair for her to sit in as she traveled.

Slowly it descended into the Pacific Ocean, expensive green light flashing off of it like a police siren as it went down, down, down. Through its tinted lens she saw broken coral with strange tubeworm life emerging from its cracks; abandoned Atlantean castles looted of their treasures by an army of Uncle Scrooges in the perpetual night; fish with razors in their mouth and ghost lamps on their heads; whales like office buildings that devoured everything they passed. The bones of divers lay abandoned on the ocean floor, strange shadows from the green light cast on unseen sands, skulls cracked under the pressure down here. She wondered about them; she wondered what had brought them down here to be with her in the blackness, what it had felt like to be them. For the first time she wondered that, back and forth between wondering what it felt like to be her, what one of the skulls outside might think of her seeing her through the revolving surface. What she might think of herself if she could just get outside to see, out there into the water.

The black emerald played music for her, sad calliope echoing out into strange black water, its hard gemstone surface protecting her from everything except the pressure. But the only way out was down. The only way to happiness was down, down to the place where at last the surface of the emerald might crack. Like a bird waking up to find itself in a shell, she had no choice. She kept descending, eyes wide and heart beating fast. Like Harmon Metzger before her, she would see just how low she could get to.

II: STORIES

STAYING UP FOR DAYS IN THE CHELSEA HOTEL

EVEN OVER THE OFFICE phone, notoriously dodgy since some long-departed Bad Intern had spilled her morning mix of cold coffee and cold gin into the receiver, and even given the eight years during which we hadn't spoken, it was easy to identify January's voice. She talked like a surfer, one whose mind had been so blown by the waves that she could only whisper like beach sand moving over itself.

Rotten Apples Press, I answered.

I think we ended things terribly, came January's surfer whisper. And I don't know why. And I miss you suddenly. And you should hang out with me today.

My boss was leaning back in his office chair. His face was completely obscured by bandages, and a dentist, or I guess someone he trusted to behave as a dentist, was working on his mouth. (Our dental plan had recently been cut.)

I need to take off early to hang out with my ex-girlfriend, I said. I'll make it up.

He let out a low moan and a raspberry stain appeared where his chin would've been. The de facto dentist shot a thumbs up.

I drove to the middle school gym where January had said her ren faire had taken up residence. It was far from the downtown office, a neighborhood full of brownstones and vacant lots lined with tires, live poultry stores from which poured squawks and feisty brass sections. I parked in front of the school behind a tow truck with all its tires missing and an angry cartoon rabbit on the driver's door: HOPPING MAD AUTO REMOVAL.

I kept my hands in the pockets of my coat as January's co-workers tried to sell me things. Spiced meat on a stick, hand-bound books, prints of women in impractical underwear riding dragons. The few middle school kids I saw were either crying or playing video games on their phones, eyes haloed in blue LCD light.

At the far end of the hall was the booth: THE FANTASTIC JANUARY, MASTER OF DISGUSE, lettered with gilt edges and strange gradient effects. The banner looked as if it had been made in Photoshop and printed off at a Kinko's by an employee who had no interest in color profiles. To January I'm sure it looked exactly like what she was trying to convey.

January looked no different than she had eight years ago. She was still tall, still with the chipmunk teeth, the eerily broad forehead, the brown pageboy. The top hat was the only thing new. She recognized me immediately as well.

You're living the life at last, she said.

Yeah hey so are you! I said. Congratulations!

Let's go, she said, getting her bag.

We went, though I had no idea where we were going. She called out the turns to me as I drove. I don't know how she knew where she was going, even; she was doing some work on her face, eyes steady on the vanity mirror. She didn't say anything and I didn't want to play the radio, something we'd once enjoyed together.

I can't get over it, I said instead. Eight years, and you look exactly the same as you did when we were dating.

Nothing stays the same, she said. It's part of a disguise. Hold this.

She handed me a slice of putty covered in salmon-tan foundation. Now her face had a hole in it, pale and lined. She kept removing parts of her face, setting them on the dash: nose, forehead, eyelids, all molded by some probably failing corporation, cheap and pitted plastic.

I never expected you to end up working in publishing, she said to me as she cleared complicated makeup from her cheeks with a travel bottle of cold cream.

That's funny, I said. I always figured it was the least worst thing I could end up doing. Where'd you expect me to end up?

Starting a girl pirate ship, she said. Working in a novelty factory. Counseling undergraduate teens to hold blood orgies in support of Satan.

Those things don't sound like things I would ever do, I said. I'm terrified of those things.

So maybe I never knew you so well, she said, and she turned to me full face. How do I look?

January looked older now, sure, but a strange kind of older: blue-tint hair, crack-vial red to her eyes, deep lines that the cheap facial molds had covered. She'd picked up a tremor that made her old T-shirt seem to hang looser on her.

You look hot, I said. You look like a bag lady now.

She snickered, her lips drawing back from her teeth like a wolf's. She opened the glove box, found smokes, helped herself to two.

I missed you, she said, factually. Everyone at the ren faire lies to you. You never lied to me.

This was true, and it had been a problem.

So why'd you want to hang out today? I asked.

She rolled down the window and let her non-cigarette hand ski the headwind outside.

Why is the ocean blue? she asked.

Why'd we ever break up, I asked her in turn.

She exhaled.

You were in love with someone else, she said.

Oh that's right, I said. I'd honestly forgotten. What was her name?

Her name was Wendy, said January. She had blond hair and thin cheeks, and she wore glitter makeup on special occasions, like mixers for the undergraduate anthropology society. And she had a stable future ahead of her. You told me all about it.

You have a pretty good memory, I said. Mind like a steel bear trap.

Only for minor details, she said.

It doesn't sound like something I'd say, I said.

She smiled and smoke crept between her teeth. It was a habit, I remembered, that I'd always hated about her.

It's just here, she said.

We pulled to the curb. We were in a strange part of town: too bright, with the leaves on the skinny oaks that cracked the pavement glowing green, and the houses were all familiar, and here were the kind of graffiti slogans that had decorated my apartment during the weeks we'd dated on the sly, that we'd sat among on the night we listened to old Bob Dylan songs together and then I broke up with her.

Thanks, she said, and she stubbed out the one cigarette, lit the other, got her top hat, and left the car. She was walking slowly, though, and I watched her walk up the sidewalk a full minute before getting out of the car and following her. She didn't say anything. Together we went up the stairs to one of the apartments, its door unlocked. The place was bare, with white walls and hardwood floors, clean, a brilliant skylight without dust in its beams.

You just moved or something? I asked.

But I never got an answer, because she'd taken off her top hat and the blue wig beneath it, and she'd turned to me and was taking off her face, too, a second layer of skin appliances. These, as I saw when she tossed them to the floor, were of obviously better quality than the ones before: some pearlescent silicon, veins and pores and cicatrices finely traced in it by some master craftsman. And here she was: hair long and black, shoulders slender, face bones delicate like watch parts, and a smell I didn't recognize coming off her skin. She looked younger now than she'd been eight years ago.

So why'd you want to hang out today, I asked, matching her whisper.

I'm the fantastic January, she said, instead of answering. I'm a master of disguise.

You never looked like that before, I said.

It's been eight years, January said. Now I'm someone you've never met before.

Her eyes were the only thing familiar, even though they looked larger than they ever had; there was some hint of jaundice and age in them, and yet the kind of loneliness you get when you're older that both of us had even back then, or that's what I figured I saw, and I tried to cling to it like Galileo maybe must've tried to cling to the idea of fixed spheres, like I tried to think of the job I'd left earlier and that I wouldn't go back to today or ever, and who knew what I would see in the mirror tomorrow.

ENERGY ARCS & FRACTAL SKIES

IT WAS GOOD THAT Sharon had broken up with Carlo. She needed her space; he'd flunked out of his quantum engineering program—what am I supposed to write my thesis on, he griped, that some asshole hasn't written before—and he'd since been bad about respecting her space. He lounged on the black corner couch until the leather balled and stank, frowning as his pixel warrior jumped platforms on the TV and dodged crowds of pixel beasts, approaching its pixel goal.

Why had Sharon liked Carlo in the first place? Because he'd reminded her of that memorable First Boy back in high school— Michael was his name—back in the days when Sharon had spent four hours at a time painting naked girls with fixed, psychotic eyes and no smiles looking out of the canvas. She was a serious artist, and she'd been in love with Michael, his jawline, his black hair and drum-tight ribs and his serious nature, and he'd broken her heart, and she'd gone into advertising. Carlo and Michael shared a jawline and some delicacy to them, some sense that they were men trapped in crow's nests, the full force of the wind so high above deck and always whacking them in the face. His face was sullen on top of the black leather couch, his controller resting on the knees of his plaid pajama pants.

Where do you think you'll go when you move out, she asked.

I can't move out, Carlo said. There aren't any jobs worthy of a quantum engineer.

You flunked out of quantum engineering school, said Sharon. So you're not a quantum engineer. You're a waste of my food and water. Why don't you get a job that's not worthy of a quantum engineer? You could make tacos. You could hand out leaflets.

In the nineteenth century I would have been a great man, said Carlo, frowning at his controller.

Get out of here by tomorrow, she said, and she went into her bedroom.

Most of her furniture was simple Scandinavian stuff that she'd bought, piece by piece, to replace the old nautical-looking hand-me-downs she'd moved to the city with after college. The bed, with its giant, knotty headboard, was the worst offender, but also the most expensive to replace. On the wall hung her painting of a psychotic girl staring at the viewer. She stared back at it and she stuck out her tongue and she tried not to hear the sound of Carlo's pixel warrior dying again in the living room.

§

Carlo sold everything he owned and he bought a lot of equipment—Van de Graaf generators, octuple-bound snakes of fiber-optic and Cat 5 cables, revolving pocket particle accelerators that thrummed when they spun on their flywheels like ancient rattling washing machines you could never turn off. He spent the whole day wiring in resistors, testing switches, putting alligator clamp A onto terminal rod B.

Sharon found it all when she got home from work at the agency; she could hear the rattle and hum through her front door. She dropped her grocery bags in the hall, kicked off her shoes, scratched one hose-bound calf with a hose-bound toe. The humming was tearing apart the walls and ceiling and she pressed her fingers into her temples.

Turn that shit off, Carlo, she called. No answer.

His room was full of machines; no Carlo to be found. She grumbled and went around yanking out plugs and breaking connections, tripping over cord protectors and shocking her fingers on clips, until she tripped the right switch and the whole apparatus went silent; the particle accelerators lurched to a stop. She looked at all of the crap now infesting her back bedroom.

Unbelievable, she said. Just unbelievable.

She went into the bathroom to brush her hair on the wooden stool in front of the mirror; it always calmed her down. There was a smear across her face in the mirror; someone's fingerprints had spelled out the word ALL. She Windexed it away.

Unbelievable, she said again.

She sat on the toilet, chin in her hands, and thought about bitterly about the meeting of the creative staff from earlier that day. When she flushed and got up to leave the mirror was fingerprint-smeared again. WALLS, it said.

Surely she would have noticed someone coming into the bathroom.

Carlo? she whispered. Are you—in the apartment?

Her voice echoed off the tiles.

Then more fingerprints appeared on the mirror like breath on a windowpane.

I MOVED INTO THE WALLS

How? she whispered. Oh God—Carlo? Can you—hear me?

OF COURSE SHARON. I USED ACCELERATORS. ITS A POCKET DIMENSION. SO MUCH SPACE HERE

Carlo—did you hear me go to the bathroom? Sharon asked.

SHARON ITS FANTASTIC. THERES SO MUCH SPACE IN HERE. THERES NOTHING BUT FIELDS IN EVERY DIRECTION. THERES NOTHING BUT SPACE, AND ALL OF IT IS MINE

§

They settled into a routine. Sharon would get home and there'd be a fingerprinted essay waiting for her on the mirror. Mostly Carlo described what he had been doing, his letters cramping as he tried to fit more and more into the limited space. (She'd Windex his words away, starting from the top; his prose would chase the paper towel in her hand.) One day he built a well of some kind to harvest nutrient paste out of the amethyst earth of his secret dimension. The next day he'd photographed the arcs of energy that broke from the rock and circled his homestead. He made lists of birds and plants and charts of all the new arrangements of stars.

SHARON ARE YOU WRITING ALL THIS DOWN. I NEED YOU TO WRITE IT DOWN AND THEN MAYBE EDIT IT AND PROOF IT AND WE CAN SELL IT TO A SCIENTIFIC JOURNAL. FAME AND MONEY SHARON FOR US BOTH

What do you even need money for, she said. Do they use money, there? Or do you think you should be paying part of the rent, maybe? I think you should be paying part of the rent maybe.

WRITE IT DOWN YOU HAVE TO WRITE IT DOWN ARE YOU WRITING IT DOWN?

At first, she did, and later she just smoked on the stool and wiped away his fingerprints as soon as they showed up.

Sometimes he'd get quiet, or invisible, she guessed, and she'd be able to pee and take showers. She was still squeamish about the shower. She'd pull the curtain shut with her clothes still on, take everything off and drape it over the rod, shower, and put everything back on, then open the curtain and come out. Sometimes there'd be no message waiting for her; sometimes there would be.

WHY DONT YOU TRUST ME SHARON

Because we broke up, she said. This is very uncomfortable for me, Carlo.

THAT WAS BEFORE ALL OF THIS SHARON

—I need space, she said. —I need my space.

She Windexed the words and stared down her reflection in the glass; she thought she'd see the eyes of one of her paintings. Instead she saw a bitch.

The next words appeared slowly, thoughtfully, like the words of God must have appeared.

IF YOU NEED SPACE WHY NOT COME IN HERE?

She cracked up.

I have to go, she cackled. I have adult responsibilities. You live in a wall.

TIME IS MEANINGLESS IN HERE. THIS IS WHAT

WE NEED TO DO IM SURE OF IT.

I want you to come back, she said. Then I want you to set up this equipment again and go do this in someone else's wall. Or a lab or something. Or a subway station. Somewhere public. PLEASE SHARON, ITS PARADISE IN HERE. ITS MANIFEST DESTINY. ITS THE AMERICAN DREAM COME TRUE AT LAST

§

The mirror fixated on its plan for months, marshaling different arguments.

WE CAN START OVER IN HERE SHARON. YOU HATE YOUR JOB. YOU CAN PAINT AGAIN. YOU DONT HAVE TO LIVE WITH ME AT FIRST. I CAN BUILD YOU YOUR OWN HOUSE AND EVERYTHING AND BRING YOU NUTRITION PASTE EVERY DAY AND YOU CAN PAINT THE ENERGY ARCS AND THE FRACTAL SKIES

I'm not reading you, she said, Windexing him. If I read a word, it's completely by accident. My brain can't always help reading words.

WE CAN BUILD A NURSERY TOGETHER. THE FIRST CHILD IN A NEW DIMENSION. WE CAN BE ADAM AND EVE SHARON, IVE THOUGHT ABOUT THIS

She started to spend more and more time out of the house. She hung out with her office-mates after work—they were really decent people, she realized; she'd always felt so guilty about working in an office for some reason. She'd drink and she'd drink and she'd dance and then catch cabs home well after midnight. She'd go to the bathroom—WHERE HAVE YOU BEEN SHARON I HAVE INFORMATION FOR YOU—and then she'd fall easily and peacefully into bed.

§

She was at the bar when she felt the hand on her shoulder.

Sharon? said Michael.

Hey, you, she said. How are you?

He was balder now, a full inch above his original black-banged hairline. It was a good kind of balding; it made him like sharper, less delicate, more solid. He was wearing a suit as good as hers; he smiled down at her. His ribs had run to fat and his eyes were mellowed and good.

She ditched her coworkers; they found a table together. She bought the first round, Michael the second, then the third.

So are you still painting? she asked him.

He spread his arms like a jovially-crucified Christ.

Would you believe—advertising? he asked.

Get out, she said. Me too. That's insane.

That's insane, he said. What a small world.

He looked into her eyes.

God—it is so good to see you, Sharon. Really. It's so—incredibly—good to see you.

What a small world, she agreed, looking back over her beer at him.

§

Small world, he grunted as he mauled her neck with famished kisses and she leaned her head back on the leather seat of the cab.

Let's go to your place, she moaned.

I have a roommate, he whispered. Three's a crowd, you know?

She opened her eyes, and then she laughed.

What? he asked.

It's nothing, she said, and she gave the driver the address of her apartment.

§

Do you want something? she asked when they had the door closed and he'd taken off her coat and unbuttoned her blouse for her. —A drink or something?

Can I use your bathroom? he asked. Does that kill the mood?

She laughed again.

Wait just a moment, she said. She slid out of his arms and sauntered into the bathroom and closed the door behind her.

WHO THE FUCK IS THAT

She covered the mirror with a black towel, turned the lights off, and sauntered out.

Go ahead, she said.

He did, and then he joined her in the bedroom.

What's with the mirror? he asked.

What do you mean, she asked back.

There was a towel over it.

Oh, she laughed. It's just broken.

She turned her head to the bathroom.

Broken, she shouted.

Michael gave her a puzzled smile, but then pulled her down to the bed.

He got inside her and they got into a rhythm, pumping the nautical headboard into the wall.

Oh God, Sharon, Michael chanted, neck muscles tight, —Oh God—

The headboard thumped again, and with a crash the painting of the psychotic girl opposite the bed hit the floor.

Shit, she breathed, and rolled Michael off of her.

Hey, he cried.

She walked to the wall to examine the painting, calves pimpling. The frame had cracked, and the nail on which the painting had hung was lying beside it. The hole in the wall where the nail had been had closed up completely, leaving no sign.

Jesus Christ, she said. Excuse me.

She took a cigarette from the dresser while Michael watched her, sweat rolling down his bald forehead, and she lit it and went into the bathroom. She pulled the towel off of the mirror and stared at herself smoking in the silver glass.

FUCKING TRAMP

Michael knocked on the door.

Can I come in? he asked. Did I do something wrong?

Sharon Windexed the glass, then took the stool she sat on while she brushed her hair and set it in front of the mirror. She sat down and spread her legs.

Come in, she sang.

Michael stepped it and looked at her in front of the mirror.

STEP IN HERE AND FIGHT ME MOTHERFUCKER IM A GREAT MAN IM LIVING THE AMERICAN DREAM

I thought you said the mirror was broken, he said, scratching his hairline.

It is, she said. I want you to fuck me in front of the mirror now.

It took coordination, but he did it, smiling and sweating from his bald forehead. She could just catch sight of the glass over his shoulder; the words hadn't changed; she closed her eyes and shook as she felt it creeping up on her. She came; behind her eyes a spill of brightly-hued paint; in her ears the sound of shattering glass.

She opened her eyes. The mirror had splintered into hundreds of triangle shards, skewed, canted in toward one another. Shards of silver glass faced one another, making endless hallways of repetition. Michael's back was repeated into infinity; so were Sharon's eyes, terrified, looking over Michael's solid shoulder. Hundreds of arms wrapped around hundreds of necks; hundreds of legs wrapped around hundreds of backs: the whole crowd of them, inescapable, filling up the mirror frame, leaving nowhere to hide. All the words were gone. She tightened her arms and legs around his warm body, choked off every last bit of open space between them. She closed her eyes, kept them squeezed shut.

TOMATO PLANTS

CHARLEY'S COWORKER AT THE hedge fund gave him the tomato plants. She'd planted too many seeds and ended up with baskets full of the things. Her roommates were going to choke on seeds and skins, their dreams run with caterpillars and nightshade hallucinations; whatever, sounded like a bad scene to Charley. But he liked the idea of taking care of something.

There were three of them, each with her own plastic pot: green, white, terra cotta. Charlotte, Emily, Anne, he decided.

And I'll be Branwell, he said. Done right.

His coworker chuckled between bites of the plates of fries that were all she ever ate, at her desk, during work hours and after them. They'd both been working a lot lately; the fund's chief holding, JJ&K, a small aquaculture and chemical processing firm, had just poisoned all the water, they guessed, or something terrible like that, so they had a lot of overtime dealing with all the new investors jumping on the low share prices. Mostly they spent their overtime listening to Spotify or applying for sculpture grants.

They're pretty easy to take care of, she said.

I know, he said. So I wouldn't really want to be like Branwell. It was just kind of a joke. You know that, right?

I know that, she said.

Branwell was a really selfish person, Charley said.

She chuckled again, handed the plants over in Trader Joe's

bags, went back to monitoring the markets.

EMILY

Emily was Charley's favorite. He'd watered her twice when he'd only watered the others once, and he read long novels to her. Looking back, that was probably what upset her.

Live, he'd said. Drink. Absorb all the molecules.

He sat on the fire escape over Brooklyn, cross-legged, shirtless, smoked a Camel, holding it at arm's length away from Emily so she wouldn't be hurt by the monoxide smoke, and he watched her leaves rustle in the wind and imagined the water inching its way through her soil, up drop by drop through her roots, nourishing her every chloroplast in her every cell until her leaves shone with vitality, beamed green healing rays into every bedroom opposite Charley's and made people forget about, he didn't know, the economic crisis or some shit, the gentrification that afflicted the neighborhood, everything bad for them.

That night it rained. He guessed it must have been the extra glass of water he gave Emily, the extra love, that plus the rain. That was why Emily was the first to die. He found her in the morning collapsed, her stem turning sickly yellow and her frail toddler roots in the air, the wind tickling bits of dirt off their once tender tips. He put down the egg and pepper sauce sandwich he'd made for himself and crawled onto the fire escape, his face close to her pot, and watched her as his wind chimes whispered above.

He let her lie there a couple of days in state, in part because he couldn't bear the thought of putting her in the black garbage bag for trash pickup later in the week, in part because JJ&K stock wobbled and the bank called him after close of market Friday to spend the weekend putting in transfer orders, making sure that every over-leveraged investment in the horrible chemical company he worked for would drop snugly into place like rescued Jenga games on Monday when money began to move again. He came in Monday at two a.m. after sleeping in the office Saturday and Sunday nights, listening to Smashing Pumpkins songs on his iPod, and fell into bed, then woke up with cardinals circling over the blank grass and dirt of his backyard far below, the disassembled pieces of his super's barbecue grill newly rusted with weekend rain, Anne and Charlotte rustling, their leaves beginning to curl. Charley bundled up Emily, cradled her sick second-growth leaves in his hand, and wrapped her gently in the comics page, washed her discarded pot, set it on the highest shelf of his closet to remember her. He was listening to In the Arms of Sleep on his headphones when he buried her in the garbage. Emily's song, he decided.

ANNE

He had to transfer his affections either to Charlotte or to Anne. He searched for qualities in both of them that he could love as he'd loved Emily's shy mortality. In the end he chose Charlotte for the opposite quality: her strange horsy determination, the way her stem reached out to the black iron ladder to the rooftop, twined around its rungs in thick healthy self-support, while Anne still flopped around alone, short and prepubescently skittish and waving her frail leaves in the breeze. Charley sat with Charlotte and smoked with his Camel again arm's length away, traced his finger up Charlotte's no-nonsense stem, and he really loved her, this *survivor* in her terra cotta pot. He guessed he loved Anne too. There were qualities about her he guessed he loved.

September was blowing in around the three of them. He was careful now not to overwater, poured half a glass only for each of them, imagined their greedy stems sucking up too much and their cells coughing, choking, vomiting photosynthetic death; he drank half of each glass himself to save them, choked on Catskill silt and zinc deposits. He read to them, avoiding depressing modern fiction, sticking to poetry, especially pretty sounding

French poetry where he didn't have to worry about whether what he was actually saying was harmful to them. They probably didn't understand French.

But forgotten Anne was the one who sprouted tomatoes first, a fat green demimarble below her leaves that Charley noticed when emptying the ashtray on his windowsill, cinders blowing back in the wind over the cellulose surface of the child that he brushed off with the tip of his pinky.

Why was it Anne? Why not dependable Charlotte? She was so much taller, healthier, more advanced—why was she behind on production? He began to buy special plant foods for Charlotte, wink at her when spinning out phonetic lines from *Bateau ivre* or *Fleurs du mal*, trying to even the scales. But the slow marble dreaming on Anne's vine was beginning to deepen, darken, and even reading Baudelaire didn't work; he found himself captivated by the strange reddening life inside of her. Something he cared for was creating something new. He was taking care of something.

Sorry I haven't like called, he told his sister on the phone. Been really busy with work. And with my tomato plants. Anne is almost ready to yield.

It's creepy that you name them, she said.

He knew that, already felt terrible, so he let her go on for nearly half an hour about the skin disease on her foot that she was fighting, how it had made it impossible for her to wear thick socks or even shoes at all without bandages changed three times daily. He let her go on while he smoked and looked through his window to silhouetted Brooklyn trees and the L train breaking above ground on its chugging path to Canarsie, all of the dark and saturated background to the red ruby that grew fat in Anne's tiny arbor, and he thought: shit, this is actually a perfect moment. This is a perfect world.

The market hiccuped again over the weekend—new disclosures were coming out about the JJ&K cleanup efforts, the stock prices swung up and down and threatened to spill hissing risk into the rest of the portfolio—and his manager asked him to pull another all nighter doing corrections. The all nighter stretched into three nighters and a half-day spent sleeping on a tatami mat in his cube. He hung out with his coworker on the last night. They split a plate of fries with Wisconsin cheddar sauce and he read an entire blog about solar conversion for brownstones while waiting for Peachtree data to back up on the office thumb drives. It rained the whole time, record rains, and he never thought about the implications until he was eating halal food on the street at two a.m. after trying and failing to get to sleep in the creaking office, and he remembered and hit the subway without clocking out. But he was too late; he knew Anne was dead before he even opened the door to the bedroom and saw the drop-spattered glass of the window to the fire escape. She was brown and wilting with one tiny red tomato thrust upward from her dying bulk like Moses floating in his basket over the rushing reeds.

His cell buzzed; it was his coworker.

Everything okay? she asked.

Yeah, Charley said, faked it admirably, his fingers resting in the beating rain on the edge of Anne's white pot. Everything's fine.

Cool, she said. So I guess I was just wondering if you were coming back in to work tonight.

Of course, Charley said. There's just a family emergency.

Cool, she said. It's no problem. I can cover, you know, two people's overtime. I was just wondering.

He didn't hear how she eventually got off the phone. He was watching Charlotte, how she stood next to Anne, leaves grimly bowed and raindrops dashing against her thick-haired stem, like a vagrant dying of cirrhosis, still pulling from her brown bag for courage.

He climbed out the window and onto the fire escape, lit a cigarette that the rain quickly extinguished. His blue work shirt was soaked through with cold and he shivered, wanted to go in, told himself no. Anne is dead, he thought. You are weak. You'd rather go inside with your radiators and dry towels than honor Anne. You're a piece of shit.

Piece of shit, he said aloud.

The tomato peered up through Anne's leaves like a firefly

deep in a cave.

He tried to light another smoke, failed, thought about his coworker suddenly, how she'd given him the plants initially, thought of her with cold fries at her desk watching money flow through markets like the rain flowing down the fire escape girders and the sides of buildings and into the faraway dark asphalt. Her own tomato garden lush with plants would even now be dying, tarpless and untended, tomatoes sagging and resting in the soft black mud. He reached into the nest of leaves in Anne's slowly cooling body, plucked the red tomato, crushed it between his teeth.

CHARLOTTE

Maybe what happened next was due to everyday guilt, maybe it was more that he and his coworker had done their jobs too well in managing JJ&K's fresh flow of investments and so stalled the cleanup that the poison had already hit the Catskill water table, deposited its active ingredients into his faucets and glasses and into Anne's soil and children. But whatever the cause, he heard a cracking sound when he bit into the taut red skin of the tomato, and the tart red juice and seeds released into his mouth like a self-administered sacrament, terrifying communion and unction at once, instant karma! There was fever in his cheeks, salt sweat mixed with the rain on his brow, his smoker's lungs and heart strained and the cauliflower stalks of his alveoli wrenched open to drink in the oxygen that was suddenly denied him. And into his eyes leaked a vision:

The yard below, once full of weeds and rusted barbecue parts, was suddenly full of tomato plants.

They were tall, winding, growing shaggy and wild, no one on the ground to build stakes for them, supported only, impossibly, by one another.

He squinted; he could see it, the plants far below growing,

thriving, living out entire green generations between the fence of cinder blocks and razor wire in this terrible place where he lived, the L train chugging irrelevantly by.

The poison rain was falling on all of them.

They were wiping off one another's leaves like it was nothing, and mysterious purple and blue tumor fruits were swelling from their vines.

The fruits broke off, rose and burst like bubbles in a dead green sky.

There was a touch on Charley's arm—he turned, and Charlotte's leaf had wound around his shoulder. Her great coughing, surviving bulk clutched tenaciously to the island of soil he'd stolen from the earth and caged her in, the withered green orb of potential pulsing and purpling at the center of her fading yellow flowers.

Weeeee forgive youuuu, said Charlotte.

BRANWELL

In his final moments, Charley couldn't have said why he was on the ladder from his fire escape to the moonsilver roof; he guessed just to put some distance between himself and her grasping thick arms; from her arms' sudden assurance that maybe the poisoned world would in the end be all right with his continuing to be alive. Neither could he have said whether he'd just fallen off of the rain-slick ladder or whether some delayed cosmic justice had actually killed him, maybe with a bolt of lightning or something. If the former, then fine: the worst he could do would be to put some of the plants out of their misery on impact, feed more of them as his body slowly decomposed there in the shadow of the cinder blocks and L train, a kind of ethical average. But he feared the lightning. Being singled out for instant vaporization, the base elements of him rising in an obscene and twisting wind into the clouds, all the chemical poisons the people whose investments Charley protected had to offer, there, hanging malignantly at the center of circling clouds, becoming fat, foaming, finally swelling and lancing and vomiting evil into the soil, wiping out all life, reducing even memory to Camel tobacco ashes as the rivers swelled with careless death and the planet grew cold in its roller-rink cruise around the sun.

Either way, impact or lightning, he thought about his coworker in the end. Who would stay with her on her overtime shifts now, protecting investments? Who'd listen to his sister as she tore layers of adhesive and thin white skin from the soles of her feet? There'd be no one.

PUTREFYING LEMONGRASS

RHODA HAD ALWAYS HAD the feeling that strangers sensed something terribly socially wrong with her, some basic hole in her character or some total hygienic flaw. So it was really cool when she came out as a trans lady and now suddenly she had something that in fact was terribly socially wrong with her, so no sweat. It was kind of political. She could field strangers' anger with anger now, and she was totally right to do so. So when she caught the alcoholic woman staring at her throat, she returned the stare like a tennis pro, held it long enough to Make A Point, then splayed her dogeared book like a folding fan over her eyes.

The alcoholic woman was with some guy, a feathered blond man-without-a-shirt in a music video from the late 1980s. He looked as if he'd been sealed in a jar of liquor for twenty years, wrenched out, and pressed clean by well-meaning twelve-step programs. He looked like he'd faded into a nice and understanding guy. The fat on his arms had long since gotten over its need to be muscle, and he left his hands on his lap mostly while he ate. The alcoholic woman surged forward into the space he left behind, punctuated her sentences with her fork, and let bean sprouts scatter from the tines to the floor when she spoke. The two of them had suitcases on wheels and wore white, freshly laundered T-shirts.

I'm telling you, people don't do no meaner shit than on tequila, said the woman. That's why they call it that. To-keel-ya.

Unexpectedly the woman turned full face to Rhoda, caught her eye again. Rhoda returned her stare and the woman smiled. Get it? she hooted. TO-KEEL-YA.

The husband chuckled. Rhoda pushed her lip out and went back to her book.

Her book was great. She'd read it thirteen times.

How many of you, the great mass of men, sweat and strive to overcome your obstacles of the day? Business? Board and lodging? The sorrows of desire? Is it not said that man is the equal to the greatest of his opponents? And yet what of those to whom the door opens, and himself he is made to wrestle with? What merit you he who, in overcoming, is—self-overcoming?

Rhoda had underlined the words twice, two different colors of ink, two previous readings; she moved her lips as she read them, felt the words in her mouth. *The great mass of people, what merit you she?*

Hi, said the alcoholic woman, suddenly standing beside her table.

Rhoda looked up. The faded husband was paying the check, arguing over what the price ought to be on one of the indecipherable items on the tiny receipt. From this close you could see the places where vast blood-transport highways in the woman's cheeks had exploded, spreading purple concrete rubble beneath her translucent skin. Her cocoa eyes seemed kind.

I'm sorry if I'm being forward, honey, said the woman. I just wanted you to know I think you're a really pretty girl.

Oh, said Rhoda, raising her eyebrows. Thanks.

Would I lie? asked the woman, and she looked Rhoda up and down, heavier on the down. Yeah, really. You have got it, got something. You look like a beautiful Jewess, like an olive.

Thank you, said Rhoda, lowering her book again. She felt uncomfortable, like the MSG in the food was reacting badly with the acid in her stomach, but it was nice to hear the things the alcoholic woman was saying. There were so few people who said anything to her lately.

You are more than welcome, honey, said the woman, and here she leaned in. Now, listen. The two of us, my husband and I, we're from out of town. Here seeing the sights. Now, we're staying in a hotel just around the corner from here. Just upstairs from here. And we got nothing else going for the night.

Uh huh, said Rhoda, pretending not to see where this was going.

So we were wondering said the woman, and here she leaned in still more. We were wondering if maybe you wanted to come upstairs with us, and have a beer or two, and you're so pretty, and maybe you wanted to let us take a look at you. We could have some real city fun.

Rhoda set the book down and tried not to make any decisions on instinct, such as saying no. She thought instead. It was strange, she thought, that she didn't find anything strange in this invitation, that this was the kind of thing she expected to happen all the time, expected it when she sat on the subway, ankles crossed and thighs tensed together and drawing goofy pictures in her sketchbook, when she looked up and tried to read the pinhole stares of the possible sociopath passengers opposite her and tried to see if they were looking up her skirt. She hadn't ever taken homemaking in high school. The Real Girls who had taken it one time did this assignment where they had to carry around an egg for two weeks to simulate pregnancy, or maybe it was childrearing they were simulating, or maybe they were simulating being ground down and trained for arbitrary submission by a brutal school system, or maybe that was just happening. Anyway, her whole life was like that assignment now; she rode trains and waited for someone to crack her egg. So all she could feel about being propositioned in a Vietnamese restaurant by Aryan drunks was relief, and with it a new sense of purpose and possibility. What merit you she who, in overcoming, is self-overcoming?

I'll do it, she announced, if you'll pay for my dinner.

The woman smiled and shook her head.

Aren't you cute as a button, she said. Sure, that's fine. Have you ordered dessert yet? Why don't you pick yourself out a dessert.

She went back to ask her husband to settle this new bill as well while Rhoda pushed her book aside and picked up the menu. In the process, turning the poorly laminated pages, she mentally tallied what she'd ordered and realized she'd sold her body for eight bucks, plus whatever dessert cost. None of the desserts were over two dollars and they were the worst desserts anyone could offer anyone. Something called honey noodles, just apple, whipped cream rice. Did that mean rice pudding? Probably not?

How much dessert you ordering, sweetie, asked the woman from across the restaurant. So we can figure tip?

Um, said Rhoda. Nothing actually.

You sure? asked the woman. You don't like anything here, we can go to the little store down the block and get you some Oreos or M&Ms or something. It's not so far out of our way.

No, it's really fine, said Rhoda. You don't have to go to any trouble. Desserts, desserts are for the weak!

The woman eyed her. —I mean I like something sweet once in a while, she said.

Rhoda stared at the waterlogged bean sprouts left on her plate and tried to decide if she was turned on by all of this or not; she couldn't tell. The waterlogged husband came back over, eight bucks plus tip poorer; he extended his hand to Rhoda and smiled.

Name's James, he said. James Geitner.

Rhoda, said Rhoda. She extended her own hand and returned the shake, firm grip by terrible instinct; he flustered.

Pleasure, Rhoda, said James. Now my wife Bethany here says you're gonna come upstairs and join us for some fun, that right, honey?

Rhoda closed her eyes.

That's sure right, she said. That's sure what's happening.

§

James wanted to go to the store to pick up condoms and batteries, so Rhoda collected on her dessert deal by ordering coffee and putting six sugars in it. James happily counted out the quarters and Bethany ran her hand down Rhoda's side and batted her sticky eyelashes. Rhoda looked at the cars passing by, carrying tourists out of this neighborhood and into other ones farther away from here, where the lights were brighter and there were happier adventures to be had.

§

To get into the hotel you buzzed a night guard and said your name into a speaker, rusted over and slicked with tobacco stains and mystery urban grease, and you waited until the guard flipped the magnetic lock. Rhoda followed James and Bethany up the stairs, the wallpaper blue-on-blue stripes and not actually extending all the way to the ceiling or the baseboards, as if someone had consistently cut the strips six inches short and decided to just center each of them vertically rather than choosing an edge and running with it. The Geitners were on the sixth floor of seven. There was an elevator, but Bethany said it smelled like urine and she didn't like to take it.

It's the thing I like least about this city, she said. It's so dirty here. I'm not used to dirty. I'm a little bit of a princess about that. You feel me, honey?

Oh yeah definitely, Rhoda said nervously. She used to brag, she remembered, about how much she liked the dirt of the city. *For is it not out of the blackest mire, the rankest offal, that the tallest tree achieves its destiny?*

Two rooms branched off of the sixth floor landing. James swore and fumbled with the key of 6L and finally got it open. *And yet what of those to whom the door opens?*

Those to whom the door opens see into a single room, a low flat bed in a very dark frame, styrofoam cooler resting on the dresser with a cold puddle on the carpet beneath it, a couple of pairs of shoes, tennis and loafers, neatly lined up by the closet, the TV left on to some exuberant network broadcasting reality programming as a ward against theft. Bethany quickly crossed the room and turned off the set while James closed and locked the door behind Rhoda. The radiators pumped in ash, MSG, putrefying lemongrass.

So here's our little heaven, said Bethany. You can see our suitcases stacked over there; his is black and mine is red with white polka dots. We call them Mickey and Minnie! And we've got the other clothes all hanging up in the closets. And here's the bed. It's a little bit hard, especially for how much we're paying, a hundred and twenty a night! Can you imagine that? You can buy a house with how much that is a month. You can sit on the bed, honey, if you want.

Rhoda did, careful not to spill the coffee and sugar, still too hot to drink and too watery to enjoy. Bethany paced, chattered about how the view outside the windows was terrible and how the radiator was strange and how the hotels they were used to didn't have radiators and those kinds of things, they had been in a lot of hotels in their time all full of big beige boxes with any climate you wanted, and James dug in the styrofoam cooler for bottles of Corona for Rhoda and Bethany, Hawaiian Punch in a plastic pitcher for him. He popped the tops off the beers and offered her one and Bethany one, and Rhoda declined and Bethany didn't. She drank, put her hand over the top of the beer when the foam started to volcano over, kept talking about her impressions of New York and how busy it was and how rude the people who drove the trains were as Rhoda's coffee got cooler and the burned acid smell of it in its styrofoam cup got more and more evident, and finally Bethany stopped talking. Her beer was more than half gone.

Listen to me go on, she said. She walked over to James and slipped her arm around his waist. We better get started, huh?

Rhoda stared into the black circle of coffee.

You sure you don't want no beer? Bethany asked. Loosen up some? You want to watch us fuck a little first? Get more in the mood?

A white pattern of something moved over the black circle of coffee, some chemical ghost forming and disappearing.

He's shy, said James. Sweetness, you're embarrassing him.

Embarrassing her, said Bethany. That's what they prefer. You're the embarrassing one. James, baby, show her your dick. That'll break the ice, right honey?

James chortled.

Break something, he said, and he set aside his hotel mug of Hawaiian Punch and jiggled his belt like a friendly Santa. He took down his trousers and his mottle-gray jockeys in one fluid grab, revealing a penis that looked as if it had been left to soak in spray-tan. He stood there, navy stripes at the top of his new athletic socks hugging his calves; he smiled beatifically. Bethany dropped to her knees and stared up at the thing rising like a gargoyle. She reached up and stroked it like she was smoothing a kindergartner's cowlick.

Isn't it pretty, honey? she asked Rhoda. Look at it all snaking around, like the devil or something. I bet yours is prettier though, honey. Take off your little skirt, huh?

I'm not sure I really want to do this anymore, said Rhoda.

Frowning, Bethany withdrew her hand from James's penis. Like water coming down from a boil it began to spread out, blur. His eyes tightened up and he bounced on his heels; he seemed relieved.

After I bought you dinner and everything, he said. No, I'm joking, I'm joking.

Okay, honey, said Bethany, slowly. No one wants to make you do things you don't want to do.

It's fine, said Rhoda in a small voice.

You sure, though? asked Bethany. You sure you don't want to maybe think this over a little bit? Maybe have a beer with us and talk and we take this a little slower, maybe?

He don't want to, he don't want to, said James, biting his lip. Sorry. She don't want to. Sorry. Give, give her some room. She maybe ain't never done this before either.

Rhoda could feel her eyes burning at the edges sometimes, and it used to be that when that happened, she knew that she wouldn't be able to cry, that she'd automatically make herself stop. But once someone forgot how to do that, it was hard to learn how again.

Oh no, sighed Bethany. James, why don't you go in the bathroom a while. Clean yourself up. Girl talk.

James shook his head, then padded in his clean socks to the bathroom, activated the fan, shut the door.

Bethany sat on her heels and looked at Rhoda for a while, the dead blood highways under her cheeks pulsing with taillights. Then she crawled across the carpet to Rhoda and sat in front of her knees while Rhoda dried the edges of her eyes and sucked snot into her throat.

Shit, honey, she said. I'm sorry. I really fucked things up for everything.

No you didn't, said Rhoda, hoarse.

Yes I did, said Bethany. I got greedy, is all. I got greedy and I messed up a fun thing.

She sat on the floor, let her legs splay to the side of her.

You're real pretty, is all, she said. You look like I'd want a daughter of mine to look. I mean, if she was a boy daughter, and all.

Rhoda didn't say anything. Bethany was looking her over.

Hell, if she was a girl daughter too, maybe, she said. You got them eyes, them Jewess eyes.

Thanks, said Rhoda.

James used to be real pretty to me, Bethany said. Real, real pretty. I used to think he was an angel, all that blond curly hair and his round little hips and everything, except an angel who was mean and smoked cigarettes and all. He probably used to think I looked real pretty too. I just saw you in that restaurant and I thought, damn, that's pretty. I want something pretty again. James, I said, get that pretty thing for me. And I knew it wasn't real, truly I knew that, but after a while, I guess you quit caring about what's real?

Rhoda sat on the bed, flexed her legs, felt her stomach churn from the coffee. Thought about how far it was to the door. Thought about how much better it would be if this woman was right; thought about how much she wished, really, that she wasn't real.

You gotta roll with what you're given, Bethany continued. People in our situations, we don't get to pick so much what we want anymore. I mean you understand that.

You and your husband can fuck me, Rhoda said. I don't mind.

Bethany scowled. —You don't mind? You could pretend to be a little positive about it.

I am positive, Rhoda said hoarsely. I'm self-overcoming. She started to laugh, choking a little, and Bethany patted her on the back gently to help her. That made her start to cry.

Look at you, Bethany said. Don't be sad. Just sit there and don't worry about a thing. I'll talk to James. We're gonna have a good time, honey, a good time.

She opened the door—steam spilled out—and she said something to her husband that Rhoda couldn't hear over the water. She shut the door behind her. As soon as it closed, Rhoda got up and immediately spilled a gout of cold coffee on the carpet. She thought curse words and walked to the trash can, reached in—hand brushing past inside-out processed food wrappers, blobs of cold sugar clinging to the exterior—and she set the half-full cup neatly at the base of the can so it wouldn't spill when someone changed the bag, by some instinct she did that, and she got out of the room before the bathroom door opened.

They might see her if she went downstairs right away; instead, she went upstairs to the seventh and last floor. When she realized that she'd trapped herself up there like a cat on a branch, she found a corner that looked dark enough and crouched there and balled up on the floor, breathing. She could just see the floor below. Any minute now the door would open and the Geitners would storm out, come upstairs, find her crouched and crazy-eyed on the landing of a strange hotel. Maybe they would be kind to her, horribly kind to her. They knew how important it was to stick together. They understood things already that Rhoda didn't want to understand, that she would spend the rest of her whole life, she was sure in that moment at the top of the stairs, slowly, slowly understanding.

And the door did open, but there were no footsteps, just

moments when she refused to let herself breathe. The door closed sooner than she thought it would. She still didn't dare leave. She sat on the dirty carpet of the seventh floor landing by a black chip of ancient gum and she waited ten minutes, twenty, a half hour. She waited long enough that it no longer seemed strange to her; she was just in a place where you sat on the floor, all the comforting details emerging: the ochre water stain on the ceiling. The place where the baseboards didn't join right below the centered blue-on-blue paper. The flake of paint that peeled from the railing, fluttered through the heavy air that moved invisibly through everything. She sat and started to feel weirdly good about herself and thought about how one day you could walk through a door and people would just let you; they would take you at your word, and how it wasn't like walking through a door at all maybe, maybe it was a diving bell, and as you sank into the ocean with it you carried a little bit of air from the surface world with you, and the more you tried to breathe the more of it was gone, irreplaceable now, and you learned to breathe other things, or you stopped breathing.

Eventually, calm or something like it, she stood up and walked as briskly as she could downstairs and out the door.

§

She checked her purse to make sure she had her subway card and found that her book was gone. The shutter was down over the Vietnamese restaurant. She pushed herself against the grimy metal door and stared through the slit in the metal at the dark window of the restaurant behind. She imagined her book sitting in there, on some waxed and Lysol-stinking table, the twice-underlined words trapped between the covers and pages like moths pressed in some collection, final product of hours spent swinging long gossamer nets in flat sunny fields.

CHAIRS

I

HER PARENTS WERE THE kind of people who never really wanted a child, but—victims of Fate that they were—ended up with one anyway. They were glad enough about it, after a while; they began to see the benefits, the hidden plusses of the whole thing. But their life was a compromise, and they knew it, and they made sure that she knew it, too. And that was how it was.

They were great collectors of antique furniture, and the living room was like a museum. They had a wide Oriental rug, all beige and purple and gold, its fibers an ideal consistency somewhere between solid and liquid, and it would ooze up around the bare toes that walked across it like ten tiny, formal hugs. They had a glass-topped table with carved swans and berries on its curved wooden legs, and a bookcase lined neatly with leather-bound editions of classics both French and English, and a grandfather clock that ticked in the corner like a sonorously snoring uncle, the mesmerist's watch that was its brass pendulum lulling observers into a peaceful sleep. Bowls of wooden peaches and pinecones released bursts of cinnamon into the heavy air at all hours of the day or night, familiar Ariels that tended to the olfactory comforts of the inhabitants while they slept. And there were two wing-backed chairs, covered in soft velvet and piles of pillows, an inviting little footstool just an ankle's length from the cushion of the larger chair where it sat in state by the crackling stone fireplace.

Her parents had worked for a very long time to acquire each of these treasures, and many hours of thought had gone into the selection and placement of each piece. They worried, however, about how this perfectly arranged life would be affected by their child, who had just worked out how to crawl on the day the movers installed the heavy clock in its place of honor along the east wall. Baby gates worked for a while, provided they were set far enough back in the hallway to prevent the whole ambience of the room from being spoiled, but this was only a temporary solution, and eventually they knew that the beautiful antiques they had acquired would be imperiled by the thousand and one spills, scratches, dents and cracks that the wide-eyed, shambling little animal they had produced would, through no fault of her own, cause.

In many ways, they considered themselves very good parents: slow to anger, firm but fair, encouraging and available to help their daughter with all of the trials and skills she would have to surmount or obtain in order to make a success of herself in this world. And they were aware that having a child meant compromise on their part, that the perfect life they had imagined for themselves as fresh-faced newlyweds would have to lose one or two of their favorite details, in deference to the third small soul they had allowed into their lives. But they wouldn't be slaves to their fate, either. Compromise was one thing, but their beautiful room was another. Yet they were confident that they could all work out a set of rules and policies that the whole family could respect and enjoy, allowing them to have it both ways: all the joys of parenting, but all of their own very important joys, too. And someday the child would grow up, having learned the importance of respecting the property of others, along with an appreciation for the subtler, finer things life had to offer, and the three of them could sit together on the wing-back chairs (they would buy a third for her, once she came of age) and they would inhale the cinnamon potpourri together in silence, and they would be very happy, all three.

So they made sure to let their daughter know, early on, what was Allowed and Not Allowed in the room. She was not to put her legs up on the table, for fear that the acids on her skin would slowly etch away the wood's luster, and she was not to touch the expensive books in neat rows on the shelf. If she wanted to make herself a cup of juice (which she often did, since both of her parents were frequently out of the house, and she got thirsty and lonely), she was to drink it in the kitchen, away from the easily stained rugs; it was better for her inevitable spills to happen on the chilly white tiles where her feet curled and stuck. The clock was off-limits altogether, although she would have loved to open it up and watch the winding, clicking brass gears perform their inscrutable functions. A general air of silence and reverence was encouraged, and eventually expected.

All of these policies she could tolerate; she hadn't known any other way of living, after all. What was much harder to tolerate were the rules about the chairs. They were so soft, so warm and inviting, and she liked nothing better than to curl up in them with her Roald Dahl books—she had started reading at three, a fact which her parents were always sure to mention to envious, childless friends—and she would hold her blue blanket in the crook of her elbow, suck her raw, red thumb, and wait for her mother to come back from her errands. Her mother, upon returning to find this incarnate threat to the chair's well-being (She would flatten the cushions! She would bend the arms!), always admonished her, firmly but fairly, to get down that instant. She asked where she was supposed to sit, then. Her mother, keen to compromise, dragged one of the wooden kitchen chairs into a corner of the room by the fire, just for her, but this was no good at all: her legs wouldn't reach the floor, and whenever a scene in her book became engrossing, she would lean forward so far that her tiny bottom would slide across the slick wood, nearly tumbling her to the floor, and anyway it was hard and cold and the unfinished spots on the underside of the seat would catch and fray her blanket when she tried to walk away.

But those were the rules, and she always wanted to obey the rules. Still, she often forgot, or proved unequal to the test of will required, and kept curling up in the wingback, whose footstool was just the right height for her to sit in comfort. So her parents took more drastic measures. They were not violent or angry people, and they never hit her or punished her, but they never failed to remind her of the rules the moment any infraction was noticed. One day she woke up to find a heavy sheet of plastic, sterile and weblike, stretched across the fabric. Her father told her it was for the best; they would have the furniture in their home far longer than they would have her, they said, and it was important to take care of nice furniture. So she sat in the wooden chair instead and watched the plastic flicker in the firelight, like the silver surface of a reflecting pool: inviting, but off limits to one who hadn't yet mastered the art of backstroking gracefully through the eddies and currents of the social world, deaf to all its caveats and codicils. It was all for her own good. She accepted this.

Eventually she became used to sitting on the floor. This was fully acceptable to both her parents: she could snuggle in her blue blanket and read to her heart's content on the Oriental rug, and there was no danger of her wrecking anything. She spent a great deal of time on that rug by herself: she sometimes met other girls at school whom she felt she could be friends with, but whenever she was eventually invited to their houses she became overwhelmed by the foreign laws of foreign living rooms, and when other parents would ask her to take a seat on their nice, new furniture, to get comfortable, she suspected that they were just trying to trap her into a violation, and one time with one insistent mother she burst into tears under the woman's constant assaults of hospitality, and the mother asked her to go home, and in the end she was just too strange to keep any of her friends for long. Her parents silently approved of this as well: it meant fewer distractions from school, fewer young barbarians coming over expecting reciprocal courtesy, stampeding over bookcases, trampling end tables, taking mock forbidden bites from fat, artificial potpourri apples. So she became used to being alone.

2

SHE STILL PREFERRED TO sit on the floor of her dorm

room when she could, a quirk that always amused the people she met in her classes who invited her over for drugs and cigarettes and to discuss books.

Why the fuck do you sit on the floor like that, asked one young man to whose apartment she had gone with her roommate and a few others to smoke and talk. —Aren't you uncomfortable?

On the contrary, she explained, this was the best way to be comfortable. She could sit any way she wanted: cross-legged, hunched over, her knees folded into her chest, lying on her back, or rolling around the floor like a stretching cat, a feat which she demonstrated for the amusement of everyone, her long body like a tumbleweed across the dirty floor, picking up fallen ashes and forgotten grit on the tangled fibers of her pullover. And it kept her humble, she added, once the laughter had died down and she had righted herself again. She had to look up at everyone, and see the undersides of tables and chairs that most people overlooked, dust-etched and gummy and fascinating, and she could never rely on any one perspective for long enough to really believe that she knew everything. It kept her honest, too. More people should sit on the floor.

She didn't think very much about this speech at the time, but a few days later she ran into the young man whose apartment it had been between classes on the campus quad, and he put his hands in the pockets of his peacoat and told her that he had been mulling over what she had said that time, that he just couldn't get it out of his mind, and he invited her out to a movie. He was good-looking enough in that collegiate way, long curly hair above a wispy string of a beard and blue eyes like Bob Dylan, so she accepted. The movie was all right, she guessed, something about artists and Paris, and they sat very close together in the red reclining seats of the theater—this was okay, she reasoned; it was a public space designed for occupation by people who didn't value taking care of things; she could do no damage here. He walked her home after the movie and kissed her on the cheek in the laundry-smelling hallway outside her dorm room, impetuously, like a darting mongoose. Afterward she touched the hot place where his outsider's lips had been while she looked at herself in the mirror, and she wondered at how suddenly that square inch of her body had been taken over, how flagrantly he had colonized it, overturned its old codes. She found it charming, in a mildly disapproving, indulgent manner.

He kept calling her and she kept seeing him; they were somehow involved, she guessed. He was a good enough conversationalist, though he preferred just listening to her tell stories about her crazy parents and their inviolate living room set, and a few times she went to his apartment and spent several afternoon hours in his stranger's bed, rolling in bra and slacks through the old sheets, feeling their unfamiliar warmth, weight and protocols against her skin and feeling the thrilling criminality of it all.

But there were problems, too. He was too needy, too sappy; he called her up too often just to say he loved her or some other endearment, so much that she wondered if he had any spine at all, whether, if she stopped seeing him, he would continue to exist at all, or whether he would just blur out, like a silver photo in the rain. And he seemed to think that she could do no wrong, which irritated her: didn't he know her? Didn't he hold her to any standards, any boundaries? Did he just think of her as some untrustworthy child to be indulged? It disgusted her; she tried not to think about it.

It stayed that way for months, and she was fine with that. He was becoming less fine with it, though. She was always so cold, he told her, so distant, and he never knew what she was thinking. He became even more passive, conversationally, paying attention to her every word with such sober nods and frowns, so intent on understanding her, prying her apart, that she grew too self-conscious to say anything, and that just made him fume and complain even more. She knew he wanted something from her, but she was baffled as to what: it was like he had given her a codex in cuneiform, which she struggled to decipher as best she could, but on some other level she had serious doubts about whether it was even worth the effort of following rules to arcane for her to respect. She began to make excuses not to go to his apartment, began to screen out a good third of his calls. She began to think about how much more time she would have to herself if she were alone, how much time she could spend reading on the floor, how much nicer that might be.

One night he called her in the evening and said that he was feeling anxious and depressed and that he needed to see her right away. She groaned, but agreed to meet him on the quadrangle in an hour. Just as she hung up, her roommate came in and asked her if she wanted to go over to a friend's house, one who had been away for a while, to smoke some pot and to catch up on things. She almost said no, but then thought for a moment and said yes. Whatever was bothering him probably wasn't serious, in the end, and anyway she was starting to think it was good to put some distance between then, to breathe (she felt the faint scent of cinnamon come into her nostrils for a moment.)

So she went with her roommate, and they smoked and chatted and had a nice time. Afterward, she was relaxed enough and the night was nice enough that she didn't feel like going home just yet. She thought about calling him, but decided that tomorrow would be soon enough, and instead she went to the all-night library, where she found a good, thick book, leaned up against the end of the shelf, stretched out her legs, and began to read, content.

Some time later, she heard footsteps coming down the stacks. It was him. His hair was wet and hung around his eyes, which had become hollow, wild.

Uh, fancy meeting you here, she said. Sorry about earlier.

He didn't say anything.

Is it raining out or something? she asked.

Yes, he said. I've been walking for hours, looking for you. I went to all the coffeehouses and bars before coming here. Then I walked up and down every shelf until I found you.

He stared down at her, at her splayed legs on the carpet. She had no idea what to think about this. She had no idea what to think about anything, suddenly.

Come with me, he said, and she felt she had no choice.

She followed him for the dozen blocks from the library to his apartment, through the chilly curtains of rain. Every so often the absurdity of what she was doing struck her, and she tried to make idle conversation so that she could stay on an even emotional keel, but he kept silent and so she kept following.

As soon as the front door to the apartment closed behind her he fell on her, assaulting the hollows of her neck and shoulder with his mouth. She was startled, and felt like clawing at him, running away, but it seemed impertinent, apocalyptically against the rules, and after a minute this excited her so much that she no longer felt like running away. She fell asleep holding him tightly to her naked chest, and when she woke up to the sunlight between the blinds he was gone, leaving her imprisoned beneath the tight-fitting coverlet in a body that was no longer fully her own.

It took a long shower in the dorm bathroom before she felt her thoughts come together again. They were supposed to go to a party later that night, and she wondered whether he would show up. She arrived a few minutes early to a smiling hostess and a living room filled with Klimt prints and empty chairs, vinyl and white. It would be strange, she knew, to sit on the floor when no one else was there, and so she perched on the smallest chair, picking at her nails.

Soon the guests began to arrive, liquor was distributed, and the conversation got lively. Then he walked in the door. His Bob Dylan eyes found her immediately.

What are you doing, he said.

Um, I don't know, she replied. Talking? Drinking? Sitting?

Right, he said, lips tight. Sitting. Get down right now.

What? she said.

Whoa there, said the hostess.

Get down on the floor right now, he said.

The other guests laughed nervously and watched. She was caught in the crosscurrent between them and him and had no idea what she was supposed to do. He stared at her for a few moments more, brow flushed, and then in four quick steps he was behind her, hands on the blades of her back.

What the hell? she shouted, and then she was tumbling forward, and her knee struck the carpet, bruising and aching, and there she was on the floor, crumpled up like a beached fish, the spilled remains of her vodka pooling around her hip. Everyone got quiet. He circled the chair and sat down in the place where she had been, crossed his legs, and faced the rest of the guests, expression blank.

I—I don't get it, man, said one of the guests.

She's not allowed to sit in the chairs, he explained.

She looked up at him. He looked down at her. And suddenly it made so much sense.

She sat up and leaned against his leg, wanting to feel its warmth against her back.

My mistake, she said.

The immediate crisis was over, everyone guessed, and the conversation started gradually again. But she wanted them all to be gone. She wanted to be alone here with him, on the floor with him in the chair, wanted to feel this forever: this simplicity, this purity, this sense of home and place, here on the carpet with the vodka and ice soaking her skirt, here with him.

SATAN IN LOVE

THE THEORY

WE'LL START FROM THE theory, painful to artists, that nothing can be created or destroyed: only *changed*. We'll apply this theory to the question of *souls*.

The one serious sticking point in the idea of reincarnation has always been the limit the theory places on the number of souls in existence at one time. The obvious *reductio* is the number of people who buy books with pastel covers and lots of bullet-pointed lists and who decide on the strength of these books that in a past life they were more important than they are in this one.

But reincarnation is usually—and unnecessarily—thought of as linear. Cervantes died in 1616; he must therefore have been reincarnated after 1616. Suppose you were born on the same day as James Joyce. You draw comfort from this. But couldn't it equally be said that James Joyce was born on the same day as you, that from your failed life he extracted the hard lessons he required to write *Ulysses*? That the literary destiny granted to you by your *shared soul* will be fulfilled by the person who, from your point of view, has already fulfilled it?

Instead, start from this: a soul at any point in space and time can become a soul at any other point in space and time.

Here we encounter a problem. In a normal view of time, every human has a unique soul. The number of souls is the number of people throughout eternity, hopefully an infinite number. But say that not every person has a unique soul. Say that every soul is reincarnated exactly once into another soul. You now have half as many souls as you do people. Suppose every soul is reincarnated three times; four people to every soul. Twenty times; one thousand times; one million times. Why not one thousand souls for infinite people? Why not a hundred? Why not one?

The theory is at once monstrous in its narcissism and striking in its humility. All humanity's accomplishments and all of its sins—they're the work of one soul, your soul, if you think about it. Learning in every incarnation, we hope approaching perfection somewhere in our future or our past. You all in the auditorium listening to me: you're listening to yourselves; you're lecturing to yourselves. Some of you think this is senile nonsense and some of you remember delivering this nonsense fondly. Some of you remember how much you hate the fucking sight of yourselves.

The bell is going to ring soon, I can see you all thinking it, so I'll close the hour with a parable.

God created the world. The Devil, miffed, visits Her to ask Her why.

God's garage is littered with carpenter's glue, insulation jutting from bare planks and designs carved into its pink crust with a finger. At its center a vast rotating globe, blue and silent and terrible. The Devil looks on it as you'd look on the Taj Mahal made of matchbooks lining the floor of your friend's bathroom.

How—how long did this take you, he asks.

I'll never tell you, giggles God, and holds Her nose with one finger as she jackknifes into the oceans around the globe. Hidden somewhere within Her creation.

The Devil shuffles and massages his temples and adjusts his tie clip. The thing rotates like a fat blue berry. Juice drips out of it, a slow greasy leak all over the dirty floor.

Someone has to clean up this mess, he announces, and after changing into suitable trunks, he wades in. He enters the phenomenal world and binds himself to birth and death and reincarnation.

One soul. The Devil's soul. Chopping the trees. Building the cities. Inventing the novel, the plumb bob. All the time searching, searching, searching for God—to hold Her to account.

Here's the bell now, so write this down for Wednesday. All of you, freshmen and seniors alike, you're all the Devil. I look out over your ugly beer-swilling fraternity faces and tan-swollen sorority breasts and I shout: Satan! Satan! Satan!

THE PRACTICE

THE DEVIL STEPPED AWAY from the platform, tapped his lecture notes into order, and gave a lazy high-sign to his prior incarnation in the front row. The Devil, sitting in the front row, winked back at himself and turned to the girl sitting next to him, who was not the Devil; who was God.

He's obviously crazy, whispered the Devil to God.

God popped her gum and stared straight ahead. Her eyes didn't match; he had told her many times that this made her look exotic; she never listened. In the collar of her turtleneck she looked like a prairie dog, waiting with its head half-in, half-out of its hole for the empty desert all around her suddenly to seem safe.

God stood up and left the auditorium. The Devil massed around her in the aisles, kept her within sight. She stepped out of the sociology building and pulled out the pack of Pall Malls the Devil had sold her earlier. She stood against a brick outcropping and stupidly tried to spark it in the wind between the buildings.

Got a light? asked the Devil. His blond pixie cut rustled past his ears and a black skirt with bubblegum trim tickled his chubby thighs.

Yeah, said God. She held out the lighter he had sold her earlier. The Devil cupped his hands around hers and cradled the flame to life. He inhaled and coughed.

Thanks, he said, and gave her a glitter-glossy smile and went inside.

God let the cherry drop to the pavement and pushed off of the wall with her satchel swinging at her side. The Devil got an eyeful: a women's studies professor late to discussion section, a traffic officer at Dean Keeton and University and another at Guadalupe and 25th, every driver in every car, the jogger who sang to himself as he and his iPod cruised past the sorority halls of West Campus, the man who picked up bottles in the parking lot of her apartment building which had eight parking spaces and the Devil was illegally parked in every one. He slammed the door of his van as she approached the staircase of her building and gave her a leer to remind her.

She climbed the stairs; she went into her apartment; she closed the door behind her. The Devil could *no longer see her.*

At times like these he liked to take solace in his memories. The time she was born was nice, when he faced himself giving birth to himself and grunted and in his mind twiddled his thumbs, and presto—*something new.* It was God, and he gathered around her, slapped her, injected her with vaccines, put her behind glass and watched her and loved her.

The time he was giving God a bath and had her stand up so he could scrub behind her knees, and he asked her where she would live when she grew up, and she said that she would like to live *anywhere else* and she sat back down in the water with a splash, and the Devil laughed, how perfect she was, her mismatched eyes and her sulk.

The times she cried, the resilience of her.

The time he came home and he opened the closet door to hang up his red raincoat and God was in there with the Devil's silver striped tie around her perfect neck and around the silver bar that held up the hangers, her pretty toes wrapped around the edge of a kitchen chair that she'd dragged in here, tough little soldier, and the Devil shouted at her and grabbed her tight so she couldn't jump and he wrestled the tie loose and it hung down the front of her, and her tears had stopped. And the Devil's heart broke because he knew that God would never let him see her cry anymore, that this was the last time; that something behind her mismatched eyes had dried up and she could not cry ever again.

He took solace in his memories because *somewhere behind the door, someplace else* she was doing *something that did not include him* and he held on to the reins of the world, forced himself to concentrate on his presentation of sales figures to himself twelve-fold and bored around the conference table, forced himself to pay attention to his hands on the drone controls and to steady the sights on his rifle, himself in the crosshairs, forced himself to keep a grip on the whole great work of the world and not to let go, to drop it all and come running to God's door and to hammer it down and to rush into her and fall at her knees and stare up into her mismatched eyes and decide for sweet eons which one was better, the left or the right.

And then he sat up and stared into his computer screens: a spark. God had posted an ad to Craigslist!

WFM 19 Young college girls brains/beauty looking for cheap fuck. D/D free preferable but not necessary. Can host, pic for pic. Seriously need to get fucked tonight so be real.

The Devil was certainly real! He cheered and signed on to hundreds of different accounts and sent her a hundred different pictures of his penis. In no time at all he checked his many email addresses and received pictures of her, *inside her apartment.* Again he drank her in: the skinny shoulders, the mole where her breast joined her ribs; he knew all of this. He looked behind her: the fake plants, the action figures, the corner of a blue couch, a green thumbtack in the wall bearing the weight of a pop star poster or a Georgia O'Keefe print or some damned thing that was no longer in the photo, that one day she had gotten sick of and torn down, and only the thumbtack was left, glinting behind her naked body photographed off-center and in bad light.

For the most part the Devil signed off immediately to masturbate. One of him called the phone number she had sent.

Hey, God said to the Devil. He squeezed shut his eyes, felt his heart swell.

Hey, slut, he said, in rapture. You looking for a fuck tonight you said?

Yes, said God. That's what I wrote in the ad.

Yeah all right, said the Devil. You look at the picture I sent you?

Yes, said God.

And you like what you see? said the Devil.

Yes, said God. It was a very impressive penis.

Yeah, you like that, said the Devil. That get you hot, slut?

Are you going to come over or not? said God. I really have to know so that I'll have time to call someone else back if I need to. There are a lot of you.

Seven, said the Devil, and God agreed and hung up.

He clocked out at six-thirty and he cruised up the highway listening to himself sing *Born to Run* and he cursed at himself in the other cars, always blocking himself, always getting in his own way. At the corner store on 29th and Nueces he bought a pack of American Spirits and a box of ribbed Magnums.

Good luck tonight, said the Devil to himself as he rang up the condoms, impressed.

I already *had* good luck, know what I mean, crowed the Devil as he accepted the change.

They high-fived and smiled huge smiles as the Devil went out the ringing door.

His hands began to shake as he found a parking spot two blocks away and he walked slowly, smoking an American Spirit down to the filter. He passed himself walking in the other direction and he nodded encouragement to himself, psyched himself up. At seven forty-five he knocked on God's door—and here was God's door, opening to him.

God was wearing a black denim dress that buttoned up the front. She didn't seem surprised or angry that he was late.

Sorry I took so long, said the Devil, flicking his filter down the stairs.

It's fine, said God. Come in.

Her apartment was a shoebox; her walls felt like they were pressing on his shoulders. A kitchen counter wide enough for one person to stand comfortably. Cardboard boxes of books stuffed under the stairs that led to a crushed-in little loft. A long desk littered with school papers and a stack of textbooks still shrink-wrapped in plastic. The blue couch from the photo—and on a table at the end of it, the gold watch he had sent her for her birthday. He had forgotten about it. The air smelled like old mice, sweat, and insulation burning somewhere behind the walls.

Nice crib, the Devil made himself say, *his heart going out to her.*

Do you just want to talk to me all night? God asked him, her mismatched eyes rolling over him.

Oh nah baby, said the Devil. Nah, I had something a little different in mind.

She climbed the stairs and he followed.

Her loft bedroom was exactly wide enough for her bed, a trash can, and a stack of books wedged between her mattress and the wall. Along the baseboard she must have taken every plate she owned and put a lit candle on every one. God sat on the bed and crossed her arms over her denim-wrapped breasts. The Devil rocked on the balls of his feet.

You got anything to drink? he asked.

Downstairs, she said. She was still staring at him. He pulled off his shirt.

We gonna do this or are we gonna do this, he said, suddenly furious with her.

It's up to you, God whispered, and the Devil strutted to the bed and he put his rough hands on her crossed wrists, his left to her right and his right to her left, and slowly he began to guide her arms apart. She stiffened her muscles and locked her elbows. The Devil sat back, *heart breaking for her again.*

What the fuck, bitch, he said.

I'm sorry, she said, and suddenly her mismatched eyes were on her knees. —I'm—not good at giving myself away.

Bullshit, he said. You not good at giving yourself away, why're you posting on websites saying you need to get fucked and shit?

Because I don't want to be afraid of people anymore, she said. Can you understand that?

I can understand something, yeah, said the Devil, *overcome by painful emotions*, and he got up and started to stomp down the stairs.

Wait, called God.

The Devil stopped.

I'm fucking waiting, he said.

God breathed. She breathed deep, let the breath flow all the way down her to the base of her spine as the Devil watched and understood just what she was doing, *and approved*. She let her arms unfold like a rose and she unbuttoned the first button of her denim dress with the Devil's eyes on her and the candles burning all around her feet. And the Devil came to her and put his fingers on the dimple in her neck that she was showing him, and he ran his hand down the lateral meridian of her and hooked each button with the bone of his finger and pulled it apart, and her skin against his hand was cold, the way God's skin ought to be.

And oh, how the Devil had her, how he fucked her for the first time in years, furious and burning, her mismatched eyes on him the whole time, frozen open, breathing heavily and steadily and without heat up at him. The resilience of her.

The Devil finished and pulled out of God roughly. He jogged in place, did a sloppy jumping jack, and then pulled his black track pants on again.

I'm gonna get that drink, he said.

She nodded, and now her mismatched eyes were closed. She rolled away from him.

The Devil went downstairs and found the half-bottle of vanilla vodka in her refrigerator. He poured himself a glass and he picked up the gold watch from the gift box on the table beside her couch and read again the note that he had written to her on her birthday.

Please come home. We miss you sweetie we miss you.

He remembered, of course, what it had felt like to write it, and *in a sentimental mood* he pocketed the gold watch. He held it tight in the pocket of his black track pants, *wanting to absorb every stray cell of skin that had come off on the metal when her fingers had accidentally brushed against it,* because the Devil knew, even as he wrapped it up and sent it, that God would never want to touch it.

I'm gonna split, he announced as he put his shirt back on. Thanks for being real, yo.

My professor said something crazy today, God said, still facing away from him, her blanket resting under her defenseless back.

What'd he say? asked the Devil.

She didn't answer. *He felt his heart cracking, and he wanted to kneel down beside her bed and let the candle flames burn him and confess everything, apologize for lying to her for all these years she was hidden in her own creation: yes, I'm the Devil; I'm so sorry for letting you down. Everything is going to be okay. The Devil promises you.*

Instead he slipped the watch into his track pants and he left without saying goodbye, *too overwhelmed by God* as she lay there with her dry and mismatched eyes. Instead he closed the door and left her alone in her bedroom lined with candles. She buried her face in her pillow and breathed her own bad air in, closed her eyes tight, *alone in the bedroom until the day when he would miss her again and he would break down the door of her apartment—all of him, everywhere; she could never get away—and they would swarm in and they would pull her down and they would make God give them an account of herself at last.* She knew it was coming. For so long she'd known everything.

SKELETON

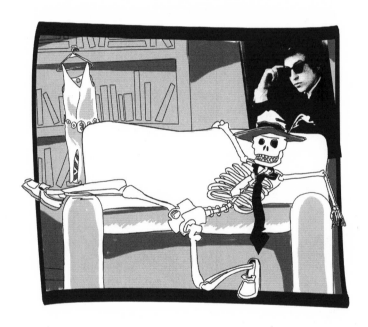

ROB BOUGHT KATIE THE skeleton for their three month anniversary. She was fifteen and in high school; he was twenty-five and already in med school.

It's kind of a warning, he said.

Katie spread the cottage cheese evenly across her lettuce leaf.

I don't know what you mean by that, she said.

Think about it, said Rob, as he rapped her on the clavicle with his class ring.

She broke up with him. Katie could read hearts, and she knew that he was just into her because she had cool hair, was weighed down by her big breasts and wide hips, was crazy in bed, and knew who Poe was, even though he didn't (he mentioned all of those to his med school friends, except that he didn't know who Poe was. That he never mentioned.) But she kept the skeleton anyway. It was a good one: Rob had stolen it directly from the anatomy class supply closet, and it had all two hundred eight bones, each one clasped to its neighbors by metal rings so thin that they were invisible, except for a faint sparkle when Katie bent the joints. It was molded from real plaster that had a hint of green to it, and Katie almost believed that it had come from a real grave. She wondered whether it was a man or a woman. Its eye sockets were abnormally large and painted a thick, smooth black.

At first she just left it hanging in her room next to her punk records and her oak dresser with the squat bottles of glitter and goop resting on top. She put it in front of her full-length mirror and watched its skinny hips sway back and forth with the air conditioning.

Kind of a warning, she said to herself. —Fuck you, Rob.

But she brought the bowl of cereal she had planned to eat back down to the kitchen, and she didn't look in the mirror again, or at the skeleton again, for at least three days.

§

Her friend Larea invited her to a party she was having over at her house while her parents were at the crafts fair in Portland.

It's going to be a Chaos and Combinations party, so you have to bring a date, she said.

Chaos and Combinations was a party game invented by Larea's boyfriend, Parker, who was president of the math and chess clubs. The game was played by an equal number of boys and girls. One boy and one girl would get together and submit the names of another boy and girl who were, it was thought, an ideal combination. The compatibility of the nominated boy and girl were tested via a number of algorithms, all invented by Parker: analysis of birth date, star sign, grade point average, height, "kissability", and a number generated via the answers to a complicated and invasive five-question personality survey. All of the calculations resulted, via some numerical alchemy of Parker's, in a single number from negative to positive five. If the number was anywhere above a two, the nominated couple had to make out—at least to second base, read Parker's rules—before the eyes of their peers. If the number was a two or below, the boy and girl who had initially nominated the couple had to do the same, as a penalty for reckless nomination. The game never went more than two rounds before it dissolved into groups of osculating, groping teens in the more comfortable rooms and people who loudly complained about how stupid the game was all huddled around the beer cooler in the kitchen. Parker had invented it in order to finally get laid, and it had worked.

Katie hated Chaos and Combinations because she always got nominated and she was always ranked above a two. She glared at herself in the mirror—her hips were marshmallows, her breasts pillows, her lips the chocolate mints beneath; her whole body was a cuddly stuffed animal for all the boys to hold and suck their thumbs. But she told Larea that she would be there.

She took the skeleton down from its hook and held it out at arm's length: it was only slightly taller than her, and looked, she had to admit, rather dashing. She took her father's red job interview tie from his closet and put it around the skeleton's neck: better still. Then she ripped a hole in the waist of her mother's floral sundress, threw it on, and in a few minutes she was ringing Larea's doorbell, the skeleton's arm thrown around her shoulder with a cavalier air.

Oh my God, Katie, Larea giggled.

Hi, said Katie as she barged in with the skeleton, avoiding the kitchen.

Everyone nominated Katie and the skeleton on the first round, but there was some difficulty in running the skeleton's calculations.

Work with me, said Parker as he punched the buttons on his graphing calculator. —Do you know its date of birth? Whether it, you know, studies?

This is taking too long, said Katie, and she shoved the shoulders of the skeleton back. It collapsed, with no resistance, and, straddling its ribs and the job interview tie, she pressed her open mouth against its merry teeth. The boys hooted and cheered, and all of the girls shrieked with laughter:

Katie, you're too much!

Oh, Katie, you're so crazy and random!

Katie kept making out with the skeleton, though, thrusting her pierced tongue against its fixed grin with a clack and thumping her floral-shrouded pelvis against its spine, and slowly the laughter and cheering died down, and all of the students went into Larea's kitchen for a drink, muttering.

With no one there to watch, the game became less interesting, and Katie eventually stopped. She pressed her hand against the skeleton's breastbone to calm what would have been its racing heart, and with her other hand she gently wiped away the white lipstick that had stuck to the green bone. Then she went into the kitchen and bit the loose top off of a bottle of beer.

That was so hot, she said. You all see that?

Larea put her hands on the hips of her peasant skirt and clucked her pink tongue.

Oh, Katie, she said. What are we going to do with you?

Parker laughed, and everyone else joined in, and the conversation turned to a group recollection of things Katie had done in the past. Declaring Wear-A-Wig Wednesday at school and honoring it for two full months. Putting on an Ancient Mariner outfit and waylaying classmates on their way into English class for Coleridge lessons. Standing along the gray brick wall of the car wash in a black bikini and screaming at the whipping blue wiper blades until her cheeks got red while friends cooed and whispered behind the windshield glass.

§

We don't need them, do we, said Katie as she drove herself and the skeleton home in her father's rusty coupe. —No we don't.

She extended her finger and flicked an imaginary dust mote from the skeleton's dainty nasal cavity. She imagined it blushing, its cheekbone flaring to baked terra cotta for a moment before fading back to cool jade.

§

The skeleton story began to circulate around the few unlucky friends of Larea's who had not made it to the party. It became so popular, so much a warped trademark of Katie's, that of course she had to do it again at the next Chaos and Combinations party a month later. This time no one nominated her or the skeleton, but she straddled it anyway and messily bit at its jaw just as the first lucky couple had been deemed compatible and the gathering of boys and girls had just begun the ritual chant:

Chaos! Combinations! Make—OUT!

Katie and the skeleton were not invited to the next Chaos and Combinations party, or any parties for some time. Katie didn't mind. She got a job at a thrift store and brought home lots of spare clothes for the skeleton, men's clothes. She brought home a smart little fedora with a tall red feather and left it balanced on the skull. She would dress up the skeleton in the most fetching clothes she could think of—suits, tuxedoes, a white lab coat, suspenders and spats, a grease-spattered T-shirt and blue jeans with a switchblade tucked into their pocket, a casual tennis outfit complete with headband and racket—and then she would play records of 1960s lounge music and put on the outfits that made her look the fattest and gave her the deepest cleavage, and she would hold onto the skeleton's yielding arm and look at them both in the mirror for a long time before she told herself that the record needle was about to scratch and broke away to adjust it.

§

She brought the skeleton to her prom. She saved up her wages for a month—it wasn't that difficult, she had lots of extra bonuses from never taking a lunch or a break—and she put down the deposit to rent both a tux and a prom dress. She chose a simple black tux for the skeleton, accented with a yellow cummerbund and yellow pinstripes that she thought would, in conjunction with the tone of the plaster, give her date a certain tactful yet bold air. For herself she found the pinkest, poofiest dress available—the bunched lace at its sleeves rose actually above the height of her hair, even when spiked—and she cut holes just below the throat line that showed the inner hydraulics of the complicated strapless bra that had come with the dress. She couldn't afford a limo, but she tied a white rose and a long stream of lace to the antenna of her father's coupe, and as an afterthought also attached four old cans on strings to the bumper. The flashbulbs went off when she walked down the red carpet, dragging the skeleton with her and smiling at all of her classmates in their black silk and embroidered nylon as they stared back at her and whispered. She waved, feeling like Jackie Kennedy and feeling the urge to throw up. She ordered eighteen full-size copies of the photo. She was so hideous; the skeleton, by contrast, looked so pure, befuddled, looking out with its black eye sockets at the prom and just seeing a gathering of people, not knowing that what it wore was a tux meant to convince girls to sleep with it due to its status and broad chest, not knowing much of anything, except that it hung on the arm of the one who had brought it there, who gave it clothes, stroked its bones, held it tight and smiled with real terror and devotion as the camera shutter clicked and flashed.

§

She won a scholarship to college, quite by accident (her English teacher nominated her; she would never have nominated herself.) In packing, she threw away most of her clothes and books, but she kept her records and she kept the skeleton. When she got to her dorm room, she unpacked the skeleton first and lay it down on the bed so that it wouldn't be uncomfortable while she arranged the rest of her things and set up its hooks. Melissa, the girl the computer had assigned as her roommate, arrived along with her mother and father, among the three of them carrying seven navy suitcases and five multicolored shopping bags full of hangers and clothes, and her mother wheezed under the weight of a large rolled rug in the school colors which she and Melissa had decided to buy while they were out in hopes that Melissa's new roommate would like it and be willing to pay half of the cost. Melissa was just at the point of introducing this plan to Katie when Melissa saw the skeleton. It was still sprawled across the bed, legs crossed at the ankles and one hand arranged as if it were scratching a nagging itch on its thigh. A copy of *Tropic of Cancer* lay open across its face, since Katie had thought that it might get bored with the tedious decorating and want something to occupy its mind. Melissa stared down at the skeleton, then back at Katie, and then she picked up all of the suitcases, the shopping bags, and the rug and went to see the dorm administration. So Katie and the skeleton got to be alone for the whole semester.

§

Katie never fucked the skeleton. She masturbated in front of the skeleton, true, and it was also true that whenever she had had a bad day at work (another clothing store, this one catering mostly to business students who wanted checkered ties and funeral suits for their own job interviews) she would take off all of the skeleton's clothes but its brief underwear and she would lounge on the bed in a slip smoking and playing records, and once in a while she would take the skeleton down from its hook and wrap its green plaster arms around her while she softly rocked. And she had to admit that one time she brought the skeleton's well-articulated hand between her legs and inserted its longest finger just the tiniest little bit inside herself, but it was too lifeless and its eye sockets stared at her like whirlpools in a black ocean, and she quickly withdrew the hand and tried not to look at the skeleton for a day or two, fretting constantly about whether this would wreck their friendship. But she never fucked the skeleton. Not once. She told all of the friends she made in her English classes this when she told them about the skeleton, which she always did within the first five minutes of the first conversation, and she was so insistent in her affirmations that no, never had she or would she fuck the skeleton (*I mean how could I. Really. That's so preposterous that I would never even think of it. I mean really*) that most of her friends stopped returning her calls after a few nights of amusement at her expense. And she kept on, going to class, filling notebooks that no one but the skeleton got to read.

§

Her TA made a clumsy pass at her when she was trying to ask his opinion on Hawthorne's symbolism, and she came home and stared at the skeleton for a long time. Then she went to the dorm lounge, took a card table and two folding chairs, and set them up in her room. She had a small tea set, and she began brewing a tall pot of lemon mint. She dressed the skeleton up in its most understanding outfit (khaki slacks, powder-blue golf shirt, sensible sandals, bifocals), poured it a cup and led it to its place. Then she took off all of her clothes and sat down opposite it. They drank tea together, and Katie lit a cigarette.

Do you think I'm attractive? she asked, holding up her breasts for it.

The skeleton grinned rakishly.

Would you ever try to fuck me? she asked, voice faster.

The skeleton grinned devilishly.

Would you tell your friends that you liked fucking me? she asked. —Would they be jealous? Do you even have any friends?

The skeleton grinned despondently.

Am I your friend? she asked.

The skeleton grinned reassuringly.

I never know what you're thinking, she complained.

The skeleton grinned apologetically.

Tell me what you're thinking, she commanded.

The skeleton grinned mutely. Katie screamed at it, screamed until her voice gave out and then kept on screaming, her throat raw and silent while her cigarette turned to ash. But the skeleton just kept grinning its fixed and meaningless grin, teeth as locked and pristine as they had been on the day Rob had given it to her and rapped her clavicle with his class ring. She was getting closer and closer to his age, she realized, older every day, and there sat the skeleton, as old as it would ever be, as dead and as outside of time.

She took it down from its tea party chair and took off its clothes. Then, both of them naked, she dragged it to the mirror and held both of them up. She could see her bones beneath the surface of her shrinking flesh (but still too thick, too soft, too much), and if she squinted, she imagined that the skeleton was covered with flesh too (like her own, but gentler, more neutral in the way it smoothed and accented its bones.) She held it beside her; she held it in front of her (covering her own reflection); she held it to her, tightly.

She put one of her records on the player and lowered the needle: Doctor's Orders, by Carol Douglas. She sang along as she pulled the skeleton around the room with her, its long, gaunt hand with its silver joints pressed into her heavy waist and its eye sockets looking down into her mop of hair with that certain look, that come-hither shine.

Doc-tor's orders say there's only one thing for me, Katie sang to it as they whirled, sending its legs out in a wide, rattling sweep. —No-thing he can do, because only you can cure me.

She dipped and its head rolled back on its neck. Both of them grinned, but only she laughed, laughed hard and for a long time.

III. MYRA'S SEVEN CONVERSATIONS

1 . RULES

Myra set the honey and jam on the silver tray, put the rooibos teabags in the china cups, and took the turquoise kettle off the burner, her cherry cigar twitching between the marble joints of her upraised left hand. She was tall and skinny and forty-three, her arms in bracelets and her legs in warmers, her short hair snarled and rising in frost-tipped crests over multipierced ears. She imagined, as she always liked to when she did any kind of housework, that rats and spiders were composing musical numbers for her; she ashed on the linoleum and didn't kick the ashes away.

The woman in Myra's living room wore a hippy pinstripe suit, her hair waxy licorice curls and brows and her skin wet kalamata, two neat gray bags only beginning to sag from the outer orbits of her cocoa eyes. Her nervous eyes were fixed on the silver stud in Myra's nostril. She looked as if she never did this kind of thing. Myra poured her a cup of tea and added jam and milk.

Thanks, the woman said, her voice a squeak that swelled the longer she talked, a cartoon mouse in an echoing canyon. —That's really nice of you.

Linda, she'd said her name was on the phone.

It's no trouble at all, dear, Myra said. Drink, enjoy. So, first. How did you hear about me? Were you referred?

It was a blog, said Linda. The blogger went on a blind date with a guy who'd stayed here. It kind of stuck with me. I looked through the archive to see if your place got mentioned anywhere else, but nothing; it was just this one little story, and nothing else I could find anywhere online.

Mysterious, said Myra. Everything is online, they tell me.

I called the city directory and asked about hotels—bed and breakfasts—that fit the description, said Linda. And they gave me your number. So I called to make a reservation.

You're efficient, Myra said. She liked efficient ones. She pushed the thick cherry smoke of her cigar against her palate, let it do some light damage. —I take it, then, that you're familiar with the basic concept of my business, she said. And I take it that you have some interest in that concept. Correct?

Linda set her cup down and sat back in the armchair, crossed her arms over her stomach, exhaled. Myra smoked and watched her.

Can I ask you something? Linda said.

The answer to that question is always yes, said Myra.

It's not—a problem for you, right? asked Linda. That I'm female. The blog mentioned men.

I prefer women, said Myra. I have problems with men, sometimes. They have problems with the basic rules.

Doesn't it bother you to have men stay here? asked Linda. Even though you prefer women?

No, said Myra. It bothers me to have tedious people stay here.

Linda nodded, plainly nervous. Myra decided she liked her. The way her hair was at the same time overworked and neglected. The way her dark eyes seemed guileless and alien, bound by a world of strange outside-world rules and codes Myra knew nothing about, as if Linda had been hypnotized by some fantastical, ubiquitous wizard who directed her on some inscrutable geas.

Your name is Linda Pallas, she said. You're how old?

Thirty-seven, said Linda. I'm a professor of English.

Do you love professing English? asked Myra.

I sure hope so, laughed Linda. I'm sure stuck with it, anyway.
She guffawed; Myra didn't.

Well—I'm Myra, said Myra. I'm forty-three. I like to write
and draw, neither by profession. Nor am I really a hotel keeper.
I'm basically just rich. I'm basically just a rich person who likes to
cook and clean and tell stories and things. I'm basically someone
wasting God's time.

That's probably not true, said Linda politely.

Let's go over the rules, Myra said. Your minimum stay is a
week. Your maximum stay is also a week. I'll provide a room and
I'll provide fourteen meals for us both, usually. You're on your
own for lunch; I usually don't eat lunch.

Understood, said Linda. My conference is three days long.
I've asked the department to give me the other four days off.
It's not a problem.

Good, said Myra. Now, in those seven days, we're going to
have seven conversations. This is the first conversation. It's just so
I can determine if you're interesting and, you know, non-violent
enough to invite to stay for the other six. You seem pretty much
fine. This is also for you to determine if you're interested in staying. You don't have to decide that until you see the room.

Okay, said Linda.

Here are the topics of the other six conversations, Myra said.
Work. Childhood. Early sexual memories. Family. Creativity.
Disease and death. In that order. I ask for at least an hour to be
dedicated to each. All right?

Sure, said Linda.

Okay, said Myra. Then, the final rule. After the seventh conversation, you and I will have sex. This isn't optional. Again, I
ask for at least an hour to be dedicated to this. After that, you
pack and leave. I'll ask you now to make all your transportation
arrangements to the airport in advance.

Okay, said Linda, quietly.

Good, smiled Myra. And of course there's no charge for your stay. If you break the rules, I just kick you out and change the locks. Maybe I keep one of your bags. I don't know. I play it all by ear. So—any questions for me, about any of this?

She watched Linda clear her throat, looking at her knees.

Do we—do we have sex in the parlor, or in my room? she asked.

I play it all by ear, Myra repeated. Anything else?

You said you drew and wrote, Linda said. Are you going to write about—about sex with me? Or draw me? Or talk about anything I tell you in these conversations?

Obviously, said Myra. I don't really go anywhere or see anyone, outside of my imagination, which I'll admit is prodigious. But none of it will ever leave this house, except maybe posthumously. Okay?

I guess it has to be okay, said Linda.

Then you pass the interview, Myra smiled. Finish your tea and I'll show you the room.

Linda finished her tea and took her suitcase from the front hallway, a blue canvas bag on rollers, a frequent traveler, in Myra's practiced estimation. They went up the stairs past the paintings she—Violet—had done in all their brilliant, gloomy acrylic. Tibia, the caramel cat, bolted from behind the ficus when they rounded the first landing.

How many cats do you have? asked Linda.

I keep it to one, said Myra.

She pushed open the door to Violet's old bedroom at the top of the landing, the room where Violet would go to sleep whenever Myra told Violet she needed to be alone, to let her feet touch the corner of the bed. Nothing had changed in the long years since Violet: the walnut dresser with its vanity, nightstand with its weirdly sensuous nouveau lamp and pale pink bulbs, string of white holiday lights long ago burned out.

This will be it, said Myra. Dresser should hold everything; use the hall closet if not. Bathroom's the next door down. It takes about fifteen minutes for the water to get hot, so plan. Breakfast will be at nine. Anything else, ask. Do you like it?

It's great, gushed Linda. Do those Christmas lights turn on?

No, said Myra. But you'll stay. You'll agree to my rules.

Yes, said Linda.

Why? asked Myra.

Linda said nothing, just let the arms of her pinstripe suit drop to her sides. She faced Myra in the doorway; Myra faced her back.

Why? Are you lonely? asked Myra. Poor baby. Are you lonely?

Linda's blouse under the suit was cream yellow, sheer. Myra scratched the back of her right calf with her left stocking.

You can't touch me, said Myra, moving closer to her. Or kiss me or seduce me or even look at me in certain ways. If you do these things, you have to leave. Until we've had our remaining six conversations. Do you understand?

I understand, said Linda, her hands suddenly in her pockets, her waxy curls shaking as she nodded. Myra smiled and put her hands on the top of the doorframe, stretching like a cat.

Then it's yours for a week, she said. On your own for dinner tonight.

She thumped the frame with the heel of her hand, twice, and left Linda to her unpacking, reading, masturbation, whatever she was into. She climbed the stairs to the attic.

The sky through the space capsule window of her attic studio was gray, calm. She turned on the CD player—*Haunted*—and took out her sketchbook, lit up her cherry cigar, tapped her fountain pen three times against the desk blotter. LINDA PALLAS, she wrote at the top of the first page, underlined it twice. She drew a picture of Linda bending down to pick up her suitcase, the work of her shoulders as she dragged it up the stairs. She was good at drawing, she knew; she could make anything look like it really looked without half trying. Tibia came up and sat on Myra's burgundy socks, kept her warm as the gray window light turned blue and then went out.

2. WORK

Myra rolled out of bed at ten fifteen the next morning, pulled on sweats, and hurried herself downstairs to make waffles or something for Linda, but there was a note on the table: Linda had to run out at eight for the conference. Instead Myra made waffles for herself and ate them all, cleaned the bedrooms and hallway, and took a very long bath with pot and patchouli. Linda came home at six, worn out; she showered and Myra listened to the water hit the tub. They dined at eight (crab cakes, home fries) and they sat down in the parlor to talk at nine.

Our second conversation is about work, Myra said. So. How is your conference going?

It's going great, said Linda. I deliver my paper tomorrow. There was an interesting lecture today, bringing *Wildfell Hall* into a relationship with *Basketball Diaries* as an intertextual kind of thing.

What is it you like about Victorian women's writing? asked Myra.

I don't know anymore, laughed Linda. I like a world full of passionate women repressed by society? All dying of tuberculosis, living in totally sexual, isolated houses?

Sexual houses, laughed Myra. I like that. I like you. I would love it if you had become a Victorian scholar to be a professional pervert. But I don't think this is who you are exactly.

No, said Linda. Um, there were other reasons. Let me think.

I empower you to think, Myra said, making magic signs with her hand.

Linda thought, a drop of golden tea spread out over her lip.

I liked the idea of being a writer, she said. But I never wrote anything. I mean, I wrote some things. Poems about women pining as they went through the grocery aisles, a poem about this girl who'd died in our freshman year. I was proud of that one, actually. I got a couple of things published even, in magazines nobody read. Then I went to grad school and didn't have time to write anymore.

Have time or make time? Myra asked.

Make time, I guess, Linda said. And I wondered why. But after a couple of years, I knew. I'd liked writing in the first place because I wanted to live in someone else's world; I didn't want to make up one of my own. So I kept on with grad school. It's an easy way to get paid for living in someone else's world.

I find that sad, said Myra, smoking. What was the title of the poem about the dead girl?

Closed Casket, Linda said. I don't find it sad. It's what I like to do.

I hate that title, Myra said. And you shouldn't write about the dead. I like that you gave up being a writer before you did too much damage.

Why do you do what you do, then, Linda asked.

Myra threw up her hands.

I'm fantastically rich! she said. I can do whatever I want. And I like running a hotel because it lets me meet people, have people to draw. And I like cooking for people, mostly. And I'd like to do this forever. So I'm very lucky.

Have you always been rich? Linda asked.

Yes, said Myra. My lover, Violet, wasn't. I liked taking care of her. She was a painter. Most of these paintings are hers. I don't have any pictures of her left because I had a bad episode one day and I burned them all in the oven. But I like to think you can tell how beautiful she was from the paintings. I mean beautiful inside.

Right, Linda said.

Does this bother you, me talking about my dead lover? Myra asked. Knowing that in a few days you'll be required to have sex with me?

Yes, said Linda. This bothers me.

Violet also loved cats, said Myra. Tibia is the child of two of the dozens of cats she saved. All of them are dead now and I gave all the kitties away.

I'm sorry to hear about the kitties, said Linda.

She was amazing in bed, too, Myra said. She had the longest, skinniest tongue, like a whiptail lizard's, and she would, my God, she would make me come and come. And come. Until dawn. I'd scream. The paintings on the staircase would shake.

I see, said Linda.

So tell me more about your job, smiled Myra. Of all the critical articles you've published, what's your favorite?

I don't remember, said Linda.

They sat until the kitchen timer Myra had set went off.

Bzzzt, said Myra. That's two conversations down!

She accompanied Linda upstairs and walked into her bedroom. Linda turned to her, face flushed, and Myra pulled off Linda's blazer, drew her belt from its loops. Linda closed her eyes and started to breathe heavily. Myra walked to the bed, drew back the covers, patted a spot. Like a Tod Browning ingénue, Linda walked in a trance, sat down with her long-lashed eyes staring up at Myra. Myra took her shoulders and guided them down to the pillow, flipped the covers over Linda's legs, pulled them up to her chin, turned out the bedside lamp. Linda whimpered.

Until tomorrow, Myra sang, and shut the door behind her.

She went upstairs, lit the candles, put on Tanita Tikaram, drew a girl sitting in the back of a freshman year classroom, scowling and scribbling an exploitative death poem in a notebook. She had trouble with the face, making it look like the face of someone who would write something like that.

3. CHILDHOOD

After Linda had gone for the day on the third morning, Myra ran upstairs, sprawled on Linda's bed, hiked her skirt, and tried to masturbate, but she got caught up in thinking about the Christmas lights and lost interest. She took a bath, listened to records, wrote a letter to herself and walked down the block to the mailbox to mail it so she could see how long it would take to return.

Dinner that night was a choice, frozen waffles or macaroni and cheese. They sat in the parlor, next to one another on the sofa,

Myra's foot jouncing as she thought about how to begin, Linda's eyes watching like a cat tracking a bird in the grass.

Childhood, said Myra. Childhood. We lived in the Pacific Northwest. It was very beautiful and it rained and I spent a great deal of time by myself. It made me better at imagining. I believe that's all I want to say. What about you?

I guess I grew up in the Southwest, said Linda. In Phoenix. I used to like to go to the library a lot—they have a very futuristic library there. Blue glass and the mountains and the sprawl.

How interesting, fidgeted Myra.

And I had a dog, an Irish setter named Lady, said Linda. She was like the sister I never had, slept in my bed every night. And I had two best friends, Brooke and Rayna. My mom would take us shopping together and get us hot chocolate afterward, even though it never got much below ninety degrees. Later Rayna and I kind of decided we hated Brooke. I can't even remember why.

She shook her head and looked into her teacup.

Did you and Rayna become closer as a result? asked Myra. Did you maybe become lovers?

Of course we didn't become lovers, Linda said, scowling. What's with you? You're squirming.

I'm sorry, said Myra. I find this conversation very boring. At least when I have it with women. Men always talk about things like hating their fathers or competition. Those things are interesting. With women it's always this precious shit about hot chocolate or best friends. Women are only interesting if they were molested. Were you molested?

No, I was not molested, said Linda.

No problems with your parents? Myra asked. No violent beatings? Never held the belt while your mom shot up?

Let me ask you a question, said Linda, arms folded. Why are you asking all these terrible things about my family? What are you hoping to accomplish here?

Myra sighed and put out her cigarette. The rain was dripping down the window panes like melted wax.

I don't know, she said. I'm sorry.

Can I ask what your childhood was like, really? Linda asked. Tell me the truth. Did any of these things happen to you?

Was I molested? asked Myra. No. I told you the truth. Violet was, though. I'm 99 percent sure.

She lit a fresh cigar while Linda sat there with her arms folded still tighter.

Violet had this unique hell of a childhood, Myra continued. Her mom was crazy—literally crazy, psychotic breaks like clockwork. Violet spent days home sick from school just bringing her mom juice, frying bacon, things like that. When the city found out things just got worse. Haldol and Thorazine and Violet forced to stay with pissy relatives. Endless visits to moon-faced guidance counselors who told her that what happened to her mom wasn't her fault. She did a wonderful impression of them. We just want to heeeeelp you.

That's mean, said Linda.

No, it's the truth, said Myra. But my God, Haldol, what that does to you. Violet's mother was gorgeous once. Then she gained sixty pounds. Violet used to love that I was bony. She used to pout whenever I ordered dessert at restaurants. I ordered it all the time, of course. I loved seeing her pout. It was good for her.

Wow, said Linda.

I think it was the coldness of my childhood that attracted Violet to me, Myra said. We didn't believe in fooling ourselves. It was a unique kind of match. I don't expect to find such a match again.

I'm sorry, said Linda.

Don't be sorry, said Myra. I found it once. That should be enough.

My family was happy, I guess, said Linda. They fought some, but mostly they looked out for one another.

How endearing, said Myra. So that was our third conversation. Next one's the hump, so to speak.

She stood up, stretched, cracked her knuckles.

I hope you don't mind cleaning the dinner dishes, she said. If you do mind, no worries and I'll clean up in the morning.

Good night.

Wait, said Linda; Myra turned. —My lecture is tomorrow. For the last day of the conference.

How wonderful, said Myra. I don't think I can make it.

Could you wish me luck, at least? Asked Linda.

One doesn't say good luck, said Myra. One says break a leg.

She mimed a leg bone splintering, then pointed to Linda's ankle, then smiled and climbed the stairs.

4. EARLY SEXUAL MEMORIES

I've figured you out, Linda said when they met in the parlor the next night, a box of feta and olive pizza with ranch dip between them. —You need people. You're still obsessed with your lover who's gone. You still live in her house with all of her things. You want to move on from this but you can't.

She crossed her legs and stared at Myra sprawled across her armchair with a cigar in one hand and a plate of pizza crusts balanced on her stomach.

Mostly, Myra said. What's your point?

This is what your whole stupid seven conversations project is about, Linda said. You need to talk to people about your loss. But you don't want to give up control.

This is such a fascinating character you've invented, said Myra. Your Brontë lecture must have been really good.

It was good, said Linda. You're not going to be able to hurt me, no matter how hard you try.

I'm not trying very hard, laughed Myra.

She sat up, steadying the plate with her cigar hand, and then dumped the crusts into the pizza box. She propped her head in her hands, smiled.

I admit it, she said. It's a sick game. But you get to sleep with me once you pass Go! So let's keep moving. Tonight we're talking about early sexual memories. It's your turn to start.

I'm not playing, said Linda.

Fine, said Myra. I'll go first.

I'm not listening, said Linda.

Myra scrunched her nose.

Your conference is over, she said. If you don't participate at all in our last four conversations you don't get to sleep with me. So why stay?

I want to help you, Linda said quietly.

Oh my God, snorted Myra.

She stood up, dragged on her cigar, took the pizza box into the kitchen. Linda got up and followed.

I mean it, said Linda. Myra, I mean it! You're so beautiful, and smart, and hurt—

You're sexually frustrated, said Myra.

And, and I just want to be good to you, Linda continued, —just want to help you move on—

My favorite early sexual memory is the time Violet put her whole hand up my cunt for the first time, said Myra, smoking.

This was actually a pretty wonderful story, one Myra had gotten good at telling over time. She'd been nineteen, Violet sixteen; they'd only just met in rival groups of friends; she'd loved how dirty Violet had seemed, like physically dirty, like she was an onion sprout exploding from between pavement cracks, and Linda put her hands over her ears and said she wasn't going to play this game, she just wasn't, stop it Myra, she left the kitchen, Myra followed with her cigar smoke like incense behind her, told Linda how she'd brought Violet back to her dorm room, how Violet had set Myra down on the bed and took her clothes off slowly, something Myra had dreamed about a girl doing to her while she sat in her lonely rainy bedroom in the Pacific Northwest, how insane that a girl three years younger than Myra was the one teaching Myra what to do, how strange and painful and melancholy Violet's short life had been compared to Myra's own, and if anyone showed kindness to Violet she would close up, only Myra understood, only Myra understood that she could be cruel and in being cruel could be kind, and so they were here together with Violet's hands on Myra's breasts, Linda was climbing the stairs now singing la-la-la in a loud voice, fingers in her ears, Myra following, talking about Violet's hand between her legs, saying trust me, how Myra had melted open when Violet's finger slid in, trust me, said Violet, this is going to hurt and then it isn't, Linda's door was slamming in Myra's face, Myra was getting on her knees and shouting and blowing cherry smoke through the brass keyhole, how scared she'd been when she felt Violet's second then third finger suck into her, how she'd felt herself stretch, wrench open, the strange sweet smell filling the dorm room, the old dirt from under Violet's fingernails absorbing into Myra's body, god, it felt horrifying, degrading, she gritted her teeth, let her attention rove around the room as Violet's fingers crashed around inside her like the Three Stooges, she contemplated faking it as she felt her body compress, crush around the dirty girl's hand, try to expel it, maybe she wasn't even gay actually, and her eyes met Violet's—Violet was crying and biting her lip and ravenous, ecstatic, perfect, eyes witch hazel and lavender and tears that leaked around the side and she still stared, so many feelings, too many feelings locked in that old, old stare, and all the love in the world in the only form she was capable of was pouring down on Myra, baptizing her, making her new, she grew, expanded, opened, Violet's fourth finger burst in, the tip of her thumb, and Myra gasped and moaned, it was like she was giving birth, giving birth to the future there pressed between them, and she came so hard she screamed and Violet freaked out and put her dirty hand over Myra's mouth and held her tight—and they both breathed heavily, giggled as the RA knocked on the door and asked if everything was all right and Myra gasped *Uh huh* and both of them held each other and giggled like maniacs and talked and talked and talked until morning. Linda's door was locked. Myra's cigar had gone out. She sat with her spine against Linda's door and held her knees to herself and stared down at the parlor and listened to Linda cry.

You can't hurt me, Linda sobbed after a while.

Four down, Myra snapped. Three to go.

She got up and stomped to the attic. *Tom's Diner* went on the CD changer. She drew a picture of Linda's face in her sketchbook and attached a word balloon from her cartoon mouth: *Oh Myra you are so beautiful and smart and sad.* She drew lightning striking Linda's head and crossed the word balloon out, and then she fell asleep on the daybed in her clothes while Suzanne Vega sang about wooden horses coming to life.

5. CREATIVITY

In the morning Myra left a $10 bill on the kitchen table under the rooster-shaped salt shaker with a Post-It affixed—*BREAKFAST*—and she scraped the glare ice from her windshield and drove to the coffee shop to eat scallion quiche and work Sudoku. When she got home all Violet's paintings were missing from the walls.

Linda was in her room, a laptop on her knees. She stopped typing when she saw Myra in the door frame.

Hi, smiled Myra. Was breakfast good? Where are my fucking paintings?

You can't frighten me, said Linda. I'm going to save you.

Myra laughed.

Okay, you win, she said. I'm saved! In five days, you and your academic job and your heavy eyebrows have captivated me, and now that you've stolen the one thing I love you've taught me a valuable lesson about how I should love you instead. Tell me where my paintings are. I'll totally love you. Why not?

One day you'll understand why I'm doing this, Linda said.

I understand now, shouted Myra. I understand rings around you, you bitch.

Linda sat on her hands and stared into the canyon between her knees. Myra sucked smoke into her nostrils.

You're obsessed with the past, said Linda. I want to think about the future.

We have no future, said Myra. All right. You want to heeeeelp me. Fine.

She went to the bathroom, took the folded up towel and the black-striped bowl from the cupboard under the sink, filled the bowl with water, took the X-Acto knife from its place behind the mirror. She brought everything in a neat stack into Linda's room, spread out the towel and set the bowl on it, hiked her skirt and sat spreadeagled on the table with the bowl between her legs and the knife in her hand. Linda stared but didn't move.

Give me back my paintings, said Myra.

What are you doing, asked Linda, voice quivering.

Wrong answer, said Myra, and she tapped her wrist with the knife, then pressed and held tight. Linda wailed and got off the bed and grabbed Myra's arm, one hand on her shoulder, one on her hand. The bowl swirled with red smoke like capsules that when you drop them in water spring into spongy dinosaurs.

Didn't hurt, said Myra. Next one might. Give me back my paintings.

Linda cried and Myra let her cry, keeping pressure on the cut. Then she bandaged her arm and put the bowl in the sink and met Linda in the front hallway, eyes still wet and her unflattering parka around her shoulders. They walked around the side of the house, tiny flakes fluttering down around them, to a small patch of disturbed ground in the grass just beside the cellar doors.

You buried my paintings? Myra asked.

Linda shook her head.

I wanted to, she said. I couldn't find a shovel in the cellar.

You were obviously digging here, said Myra.

I tried to use my hands, said Linda. It was too cold.

Myra stared at her.

Let me see your fingers, she said.

She didn't wait for Linda, just grabbed her arms and pulled her mittens off. Dirt and scabs and blood on the ridges of her fingertips. Myra closed her eyes and put Linda's hands into her mouth. Linda whimpered.

They retrieved the paintings from the cellar, and Myra heated the milk for cocoa while Linda sat, staring, in the armchair.

Maybe there's more to you than I gave you credit for, sang Myra. I love that you tried to bury the paintings with your bare hands. That's something Violet might have done. I'm excited. I don't know what's going to happen.

Please never compare me to Violet, Linda said, monotone.

Now that is hardly the way to Myra's heart, said Myra. Drink this, and I'll show you all the paintings. If you love me, I want you to love them.

I love you, said Linda. Not the paintings, or Violet. I think Violet was a very fucked-up person.

This was one of her early pieces, said Myra, picking up the first canvas. —Juvenile, but what can you do; she died young.

Linda stood up, leaving her cocoa on the table.

I'm not going to listen to this, she said. Good night.

She walked upstairs. Myra set the painting down and picked up Linda's cup. She stared at the contents of it for a while, sloshed them around, decanted the contents into her own cup, mixed them, drank. She went upstairs and knocked on Linda's door.

Please go away, Linda said.

I can't love anyone, Myra said. But if I could love anyone, it'd be you. Probably. I think.

Linda opened the door, eyes wet, her pajamas covered with Irish setters.

Come finish our conversation, Myra said. I want to finish our conversation.

This is hurting me, Linda said. I'm leaving here in the morning. Good night.

She stared to close the door. Myra thought about wedging her foot in it, the side of her stocking shredding on Linda's closing door, what it might feel like to do that. She stared a while, then went downstairs and washed the cocoa things, mouth still tasting the dirt in the ridges of Linda's fingers.

6. FAMILY

She set an alarm that night, and good thing she did; she had just made it down the stairs, the cab honking outside, in her plaid bathrobe to find Linda with her bags packed and waiting by the door.

It was wonderful meeting you, Linda said.

No it wasn't, said Myra. Obviously it wasn't.

Linda's eyes grew sad. She turned and picked up her suitcase.

Goodbye, she said over her shoulder, and she walked to the cab. The sky was swirling with gray and storm. Myra followed, stood on the porch, ends of her robe lashing against her legs.

You're never going to forget me, she shouted. We have unfinished business.

Goodbye, Linda called, and she got into the cab and disappeared.

Myra went inside, sat in her armchair with her legs up on the hassock, let her robe hang open, smoked and stared at the stucco on the ceiling. Tibia got onto the armrest and she pushed her aside, got up and found the Yellow Pages, looked under Hotels & Motels.

Paterson Ramada, said the concierge at the other end of the first listing.

I was wondering, said Myra. Do you have a guest registered named Linda Pallas? If you do, could you leave her an important message?

I'm not sure, ma'am, said the concierge. I could check. Would you mind giving me the message?

But of course not, said Myra. Okay. Conversation six: family. As I've said, my family was very distant, which was hard as a young girl. Violet could see it right away, the first time she came with me to visit my hometown—

The concierge hung up. Myra screamed and slammed the phone receiver down four times, then tore the page out of the phone book and crushed it.

She couldn't write or draw and every CD she tried to listen

to disgusted her. She forgot to eat until late. After finishing a quarter bowl of instant soup she stared into space, and then she took Violet's paintings and put them into the crawl space under the stairs. Tibia yowled at her feet, hungry. She thought about nothing and finally went back into the closet and took out a sleeping bag and two afghans, still in her robe. She took off her robe, folded it, set it on the steps, and went out to the porch. Snow was on the grass all around, more of it blowing in, and she could feel her skin crawl and tighten, laughed at herself. What would this feel like? She wrapped herself in the sleeping bag, covered herself with the afghans; her vision swam.

7. DISEASE AND DEATH

She knew that if anyone found her it would be Linda, knew it as soon as she felt Linda's hand on her frozen shoulder, saw the dark eyes above her, her curls haloed in the yellow porch light against the black midnight sky.

Hiiii, Myra sang, and her eyes closed again.

She was hazy on exactly how Linda got her upstairs, the afghan around her shoulders, but she must have at least been semiconscious. There was no way Linda would have decided on her own, without Myra's insistence, to bring her to the attic. She lay on the daybed, Linda going through the CD collection. She put on Sonic Youth, Thurston Moore singing about his dead insane sister.

Good choice, said Myra. You have some taste.

Thanks, said Linda. Are these your drawings? They're wonderful.

Be careful, said Myra. Some of them are of you.

I won't look, said Linda, closing the sketchbook.

I hate cowards, said Myra.

Outside the tiny window everything remained black, as if the house were a space capsule hurtling in eerie orbit around a dark moon, the sun not close enough to warm them but close enough to smear out the light of other stars.

Why did you do it, Linda asked.

Myra frowned, then realized what she was getting at.

You think it was some kind of suicide attempt? Myra asked. That's ridiculous. You're such an English professor.

Myra, you didn't even have clothes on, said Linda. I—I tried to call from the hotel. I was worried. When I couldn't reach you I took a cab so I could check on you.

I had a sleeping bag, Myra snarled.

They sat there while the wind and Kim Gordon sang about angels.

I don't know why I did what I did, said Myra. I don't know.

Was it because of Violet? asked Linda.

She was crying, and Myra watched the streaks of her tears like comets in the black window; Myra watched them and imagined drawing her face, and something was wrong because she couldn't imagine where the lines were meant to go. And what she wanted to do, really, was to draw the invisible thing behind Linda's face, the thing she could suddenly feel, thought she could feel, the same way she felt gravity, air pressure, her own beating heart—all things imperceptible until she let herself perceive them. And if she drew every day for a thousand years she knew she could never draw that thing. Violet could never have drawn it either. She started to cry.

What's wrong, cried Linda.

I don't know what's wrong with me, sobbed Myra, —I'm so horrible, I'm so horrible—

Linda clambered onto the daybed with her, pushed her shoulders down; Myra didn't resist—Linda lay down beside her, her breasts pressing into Myra's back, Myra sobbed and a strange dead sound rose from her throat as the CD shifted into the horrible Ciccone Youth song that closed the album and Linda stretched out to turn it off and there they were in silence.

I don't know why I wasn't enough for her, sobbed Myra, —I don't know why we're so disgusting, I hate her so much, I hate her—

Calm down, said Linda. You have to calm down—

Why are you so nice to me? Myra asked.

She sat up, sniffed; Linda lay on the bed; Myra propped herself over her.

Why? she demanded. Why are you so nice to me? What makes you so special—

Linda pulled her down, pushed her whole head back with her kiss; she could feel a dark heat like cosmic rays, solar wind; she surged forward, kissed Linda back.

8. THE FUTURE

They worked their clothes off; Myra laughed at Linda's orange underwear with the Jack-o-lantern smile across the ass, Linda wrestled her down and told her she was no longer allowed to make fun, yet when Myra touched her, her face went longing and blank except for bright glowing insane eyes under dark lowering eyebrows, and when Linda rose up and forced Myra down and let her curls drift down Myra's stomach and asked *is it all right* and Myra said *of course it's fucking all right* and then suddenly sucked in breath and screamed as Linda was suddenly everywhere, filled up all points of space.

The sun rose and turned the sky through the space capsule window purple, promising.

Let's join a marathon, said Myra. Let's buy a hot air balloon. Let's become the champion welterweight boxers of North America.

Linda nestled her cheek and her sour breath into Myra's freckled shoulder. —What time is it?

Maybe seven, said Myra. Let me get up. I have to make breakfast.

Don't leave me, said Linda, rolling over then falling asleep. Myra watched her.

I'll make breakfast, she said to Linda's sleeping back. —You love breakfast. She walked downstairs, Tibia dancing in her wake, found her plaid bathrobe by the stairs and put it on, looked out the front windows. The snow had broken into rain; she listened to it as it melted the ice on the branches in cracks. She made her phone call, and she simmered spinach and lemon juice for savory crepes. She made potato galettes to go with the crepes, pulled strawberries from the freezer and swirled them into fresh cream, heated miniature quiches with fontina and bacon, ladled red current jam into a gravy boat, set teabags in cups waiting for the boiling water to unlock them. The tea was whistling when Linda came down the stairs in Myra's college T-shirt and an old pair of Violet's boxers, blinking her way into the kitchen.

Oh my God, she said. Is this all for me?

And me and Tibia, said Myra. It's not just you in the world.

She held the chair for Linda and sat opposite, poured coffee from a French press, smiled lazily at Linda over the rim of her glass.

This is nice, Linda said. You're nice to me sometimes.

I'm glad you like the food, smiled Myra.

I like the food, said Linda. I'm in love with you.

Thank you, said Myra. She sat back, stretched, lit her cigar. Come on, eat, eat. There's only an hour or so left before your airport shuttle gets here.

Linda blinked, swirled up strawberries.

I don't need a shuttle, she said. I already decided to change my ticket. I have some vacation time coming up; I want to spend it here with you. I want to see where things go.

Myra said nothing.

We have a lot to talk about, don't we? asked Linda, voice raising.

No, said Myra. We're done talking. We've already had our seven conversations.

Linda put down her strawberry spoon. Myra sighed and drummed her fingers on the table.

We also had the sex, of course, she said.

We never had a seventh conversation, said Linda, her voice suddenly quiet. —Or a sixth.

Please eat, said Myra. Please believe that I know how hard this is.

Linda said nothing, just let her strawberry jam leak from spoon to tablecloth.

The least you could do is eat my food, Myra said. Then I won't feel so terrible.

I hate you, said Linda.

Everyone says that, said Myra. But I told you exactly what would happen. That's exactly what happened.

That's not true, said Linda, and suddenly she was on her feet.

You made me love you too, said Myra. It doesn't work otherwise. It isn't real.

She knew Linda was going to storm away from the table; everyone did. She followed her up the stairs to the attic. She watched Linda re-button the jacket she'd buttoned up wrong, listened to her curse. She felt like a child in an inner tube spinning on the surface of feeling. She wished the tube wasn't so thick, wished her arm was long enough so that her hand could reach, penetrate the water.

Look, I'm sorry, Myra said. I really am.

Don't fucking talk to me, Linda said.

You're going to feel better about this, said Myra. You're going to forget about me. It's better if you do. I like being this way. You got closer than anyone else has. Do you realize that?

Get out of my way, Linda said. I'm not waiting for the shuttle.

Myra moved aside, crouched on the landing with Tibia, and smoked and watched Linda zip her terrible parka and check her curls in the mirror by the door that led to winter and rain. This was always the worst moment, the beginning of winter, of doubt, recrimination. Then she'd start to wake up in the spring, feel like Myra again in the summer, begin to think about Violet again in the fall. Her heart would empty again and only seven conversations would bring her back to life. Linda hated her? Linda had it easy. If Linda ran out of fuel she could read a novel or fall in love or something, pump herself full of emotional gasoline. Myra and Violet had never had it easy. Myra and Violet had to live in the way only they could: to accept everything for what it was, feed on it in whatever way they could, do what it took to stay alive after feeling was dead, and feeling always died. Violet had never learned how to stay alive like this, and Myra had. She felt a little sorry for Linda as she sat, the shock of teardust on her cheekbones and her cherry cigar burning and Tibia's scruff rustling. Linda would never learn what Myra had to learn. Linda would always find it easy to be alive.

She turned before she went out the door, eyes shining bright out of her brows' shadow.

Please let someone make you happy, she said.

The door closed behind her. Myra sat with her hand still on Tibia's fur.

She went to the attic and opened the sketchbook. The page was white. Suddenly she could see it, where the black lines ought to go, the secret contours of the thing behind Linda's face. She fell on the floor and wailed in a rusted voice and shut her eyes, the better to stop seeing the invisible contours that filled the page, waiting for her pen to follow them.

Austin & New York, 2006–2014

ACKNOWLEDGEMENTS

The stories in this book were written over something like an eight year period, so it's essentially impossible to thank everyone who really ought to be thanked. But good starting points may include: Fiction Circus, KGB Lounge, Meredith Dawson, John Oakes, OR Books, Dylan Edwards, Geoff Sebesta and Gewel Kafka, Lilana Wofsey Dohnert, Antioch University, Veronica Liu, Jason Laney, Jim Feast, Barney Rosset, Colin Meldrum.

The best of all thanks though to Miracle Jones, Kevin Carter, Chavisa Woods, Bill Cheng, Joseph Sachs, Kathleen Jacques, Anton Solomonik.

Wren Hanks: the part about the horrible angler fish is for you. <3

ABOUT THE AUTHOR

JEANNE THORNTON is the author of *The Dream of Doctor Bantam*, a Lambda Literary Award finalist, and the creator of the webcomics *Bad Mother* and *The Man Who Hates Fun*. She is the editor, with Tara Avery, of the trans comics anthology *We're Still Here*, and along with Miracle Jones, she is one of the founders of Instar Books. She lives in Brooklyn.